STARTING AGAIN

Under witness protection and relocated with a new identity, Clare Rayne cannot release her fear of the past — until Blake Fielding pulls up in her driveway, calmly announces he knows about her and will be staying in the cabin next door. Clare discovers Blake is a counsellor sent to help her and, as they work together, they fall in love. But Blake resists involvement and leaves when their consultations are complete. Will he return, or must Clare face her future alone?

NOELENE JENKINSON

STARTING AGAIN

Complete and Unabridged

LINFORD
Leicester

First published in Great Britain in 2002

First Linford Edition
published 2004

British Library CIP Data

Jenkinson, Noelene
    Starting again.—Large print ed.—
Linford romance library
    1. Witnesses—Protection—Fiction
    2. Love stories 3. Large type books
    I. Title
    823.9'14 [F]

    ISBN 1–84395–161–4

Published by
F. A. Thorpe (Publishing)
Anstey, Leicestershire

Set by Words & Graphics Ltd.
Anstey, Leicestershire
Printed and bound in Great Britain by
T. J. International Ltd., Padstow, Cornwall

This book is printed on acid-free paper

1

Clare Rayne braved standing outdoors in the frosty morning but stayed close enough to Cabin Two for retreat. The surface of the sheltered Gippsland Lake in Australia's Southern Victoria on her doorstep was dark and hugged by a layer of fog.

She breathed deeply, inhaling the scent of woodsmoke. Resident for over a month, she hadn't yet mustered the courage to visit the township nestled into the half-circle curve of the low, wooded hills across the still water on the opposite shore.

Troubled by an unshakeable fear, and so far unable to change the situation, she avoided people and stayed safe. But twiddling her thumbs was grating on her nerves and the need for isolation had worn thin. She stiffened as the sound of a vehicle echoed around the lake road, shattering the peace. Arrivals in this secluded area were rare and therefore suspect. Clare panicked that they had discovered her and she would die. In a brief flash of reason, she wondered if they would seek her in daylight.

Now invaded, she froze. Her heart lurched in fright when the four-wheel drive turned into the short, unsealed track that led to her cabin. Dan had assured her this was a safe house, true so far, but familiar feelings of alarm resurfaced as the vehicle pulled up barely yards away.

A tall man slammed the door and started towards her. Cushioned by a thick bed of damp leaves, his brown boots made a soft thud as he approached. He looked decent enough but you never could tell. Anatole Guzzi had looked nice enough, too.

Clare tensed and prepared warily to meet him. On principle, since the recent upheaval in her life, she trusted no-one. The intruder cast a subtle but curious look around as he closed the distance between them. His actions were unusual, guarded, as though he knew exactly what he was doing and what he sought. Clare wasn't given a chance to dwell on his behaviour, however. At the precise moment he reached her, the man's big brown eyes sparkled and his mouth exploded into a slow, disarming smile. Clare forgot everything and gulped. This kind of man drew women to him. She eyed him up and down again, confirming her initial appraisal. He might even appeal to her, too, one day, if she ever trusted men again.

He blew on his hands and rubbed them together.

'Hi.'

The voice was rich and deep, and as smooth as the surface of the lake.

Unsmiling, she blurted out, 'Lost?'

Her crisp tone told him he was unwelcome. Apart from her regular grocery order by telephone, this was the first outsider she had spoken to in weeks.

'I'm looking for Cabin Three,' he said, his smile dimming.

He would be her neighbour? She hoped he kept to himself.

'Next one along. People around here keep to themselves.'

Amused rather than rejected, he thrust out a big hand toward her.

'Blake Fielding.'

She kept her hands down and nodded.

'Clare Rayne.'

Her voice trembled. It wasn't her real name, of course, but she would never risk using that again.

'I know.'

Clare's mind froze in fear and she glared at him. He knew her? Was he out to get her, after all? Gain her trust then pounce?

'What!'

'Better get used to having me around. I'll be checking on you every day.' he said with dry humour, moving off toward his vehicle.

Clare's feet galvanised into action. As

she strode after him the cold, morning air stung her face.

'Who sent you?' she asked, her voice trembling slightly.

'A friend.'

'You could be anybody. Where's your identification?'

'Relax, I won't hurt you.'

Clare halted and stared. Dan must have told him, but why? Oddly, she found his silky reassurance calming. So far, he hadn't attempted to harm her. All the same, caution had become second nature. As he slid behind the wheel, Clare grabbed the open door.

'I don't know that.'

Fielding's gaze warmed.

'Trust me.'

'I can make a phone call and check you out.'

'Feel free.'

Maybe he had nothing to hide after all. Although her past was a stolen memory and her future unsettled, Clare had found refuge here, a peaceful haven, a no-man's land of respite between the two. Unable to go back but afraid to go on, she felt safer until now. She fought off rising anxiety that eventually she must recognise the outside world but didn't want to. It seemed too soon.

'I want to be left alone.'

'Honey,' Fielding's voice grew crisp, 'right about now I should be on a warm, Greek island, some place in the Mediterranean.'

'Then why aren't you?' she snapped, offended by the regret in his voice.

'A man has to eat.'

'Great! You're only interested in money.'

Once, she had been, too, and felt guilty for the accusation.

'I've been hired for a month, whether you approve or not.'

'I don't!'

'See you around,' he said and flashed a careless smile.

He reversed from her driveway and disappeared from sight. Cabins Two and Three were only separated by a few hundred metres of bushland. She couldn't see him but would know he was there and stay alert. His reason sounded genuine enough but she planned to check.

Long strides carried her up the cabin steps, across the veranda and inside. She kicked off her sneakers and headed for the telephone, punching in a safety code before the numbers. There was a time limit and she would need to keep it short. When Dan, her case officer, answered, Clare skipped a greeting and jumped straight to the point.

'What on earth do you think you're doing?'

A lapse occurred before he responded. 'Fielding's arrived?'

'You didn't warn me.'

'Your phone didn't answer.'

Clare sighed. Sometimes, over anxious, she unplugged it. She wished it would ring yet grew fearful on the rare occasion it did.

'You're still strung up, so I've hired Fielding for you,' Dan said.

'To do what?'

'Talk.'

'I've told you before, don't push. Send him away,' she demanded. 'I'll decide soon but in my own time and at my own pace, OK?'

'Your pace always used to be supersonic, kiddo.'

'I'm being careful. I want to make the right choices.'

Clare paced with the cordless phone. For safety before the trial, she had been constantly moved around. Afterwards, she had just wanted stability and quiet. But instead of getting out and starting again, she had fallen into a heap. She understood Dan's insinuation. Hibernation was comforting but aimless.

'I'll get around to it,' she said.

'You know the drill. You should be independent by now.'

'I will be but — '

'No buts. Trial's finished and Guzzi's doing time. There's minimal danger now. Give Fielding a chance. Not all men are jerks and he can help you. He's a counsellor.'

'A shrink!'

Dan chuckled.

'A qualified friend.'

'You think I'm nuts!'

'You've been under a big stress. You should talk to this guy.'

'If I need conversation, I'll go out and look.'

'You haven't yet.' He sighed. 'You're a clever woman, Clare. Accept a little well-intentioned help, OK?'

'Dan, I . . . '

'Gracefully!' he cut in.

Clare closed her eyes and heaved a long, shaky sigh of frustration. Dan only wanted what was best for her. Hadn't she trusted him with her life all through the trial, and been welcomed and included into his family without question? Dan wouldn't lie and she owed him a hundred favours.

Clare felt caught amid uncompromising stubbornness, obligation in the face of his gesture and guilt at her inability to progress. Two years ago she had been a confident and successful business woman.

'All right. You win. But if it doesn't work out,' she added, 'Fielding goes.'

'No problem, but give the guy a decent break first.'

'Promise.'

Running short of time, Clare groped for words to change the subject.

'How's the family.'

'Mary and the boys are just fine.'

Clare's throat went dry and she wanted to weep, an inclination, despite her constant fear and loneliness, to which she rarely succumbed. Dan and Mary had supported her through everything.

After her life blew up in her face, she'd had to leave her old one behind, her parents, friends, two siblings and beloved dog. Alone and afraid, she was supposed to start with a new life and identity but she didn't even know who this new woman, Clare Rayne, was yet. With caution, she was free to go anywhere, including Melbourne, but was terrified to take that first step.

'Give my love to them all,' her voice quavered.

'Will do.'

' 'Bye, Dan.'

'Take care.'

She cringed as she hung up. Did he have to phrase it quite like that? She crossed the living-room to the wide, picture window and looked out across the lake. The fog had thinned.

After the trial, she had innocently presumed that the nightmare would end but it persisted, at least in her mind. Clare felt frustrated by its depth of emotional control. Toley's invisible tentacles still reached out and had her in their grip. She despised him for the unwanted legacy, helpless at her inability to overcome it. She so wanted to but didn't know how to begin.

She wished Dan hadn't created new pressure from this Fielding guy. It rattled her security. She didn't know a thing about him.

Within an hour, Clare's opportunity to have her curiosity satisfied came sooner than expected. Staring into the fireplace flames wishing she could tell this man to leave, she heard footsteps outside. The wire screen door whined and the front door opened. Blake Fielding was back. He didn't bother to knock, just barged in and closed the door against the cold.

Panicking at his intrusion, Clare's heart beat faster. Even as he moved into the compact living-room with its comfortable sofas, deep chairs and bookshelves, his sharp gaze, cool and complete, swept his surroundings as he had done earlier outdoors, as though filing away every detail for future reference. Awed by his presence, Clare didn't know whether to feel protected or terrified. Since Dan had verified him, she relaxed.

When her pulse slowed, she said, 'You've already checked on me today.'

He shrugged and moved closer to the fire, extending his hands to the warmth.

More composed, Clare studied him. He was roughly handsome with a great mop of dark brown hair, every strand of which did exactly as it pleased. He looked ruffled and appealing and strong, the kind of person to whom you would trust your life. Affected by his daunting charisma, she moved into the kitchen to make coffee.

'I take mine black, two sugars,' he called out.

'Perhaps you'd care to get it yourself.'

She threw him a sweet smile when she returned carrying her own steaming mug and sitting in her favourite chair by the open fire. He was settled on the sofa, flipping through a National Geographic magazine.

She avoided his gaze. When she had first encountered his dark eyes, they had drawn her in. Toley's black eyes had done the same and she refused to succumb again, not in this lifetime.

Unperturbed by her lack of hospitality, Blake rose and disappeared into the timber and white galley kitchen, made himself coffee and returned to the lounge. Clare suffered a twinge of resentment at his ease.

'You're on one cup a day and thirty minutes' conversation,' she said.

'Ground rules, huh?' He grinned. 'I'll take it.'

After minutes of unnerving silence, broken only by an occasional spit and crackle from the fire, and the muted sound of the ferry horn as it departed for another lake crossing, Clare squirmed, secretly plotting Dan's revenge for inflicting this man upon her. She cupped her hands around the mug and sipped, keeping her eyes averted.

Lounging and casual, Fielding studied the woman's tense body language. Dan was right. She sure needed help. Facing it would be her biggest hurdle. After that, it should be an easy ride. Dan had explained her situation, all about the trial, the national media coverage of every sensational detail. Blake had cursed when he and his

14

partner, Mac, had tossed for this job and he won. The chance to sun himself for a few weeks on a Greek island slipped through his fingers. Babysitting, that's what he thought he'd be doing, but since seeing Clare, he changed his mind. He liked what he saw. What breathing man wouldn't? She was striking.

Tousled, highlighted hair the colour of vintage brandy swirled around her shoulders. Her mouth, devoid of lipstick, was lush red and generous and lured his imagination on to dangerous ground. She was tall. When they had first met, her gaze had been only inches lower than his own. Blake sighed. Pity he never mixed business with pleasure.

'You promised me a half hour of conversation.'

Startled by Blake's voice, Clare jumped. She hastily brushed at the brown drops of spilled coffee, grateful that her sweater was old and a dark colour.

15

'About what?''

He watched her, his gaze annoyingly inscrutable.

'You.'

After Toley's betrayal, it was a big request. Yet she sensed this man had the power to achieve it. The thought terrified her. So far she had kept everything bottled inside. The thought of disclosure was alarming.

'Afraid?' he asked.

Her head whipped up at his soft taunt.

'Of what?'

'Talking.'

Clare moved uncomfortably in her chair. If she was as clever as Dan claimed, why had she agreed to this? Wounds, when opened, hurt.

'I'm not crazy. I don't need any of this.'

'I know. You're intelligent and mature. You just need to offload. Apparently you haven't confided in anyone. So talk.'

'You first,' she countered.

If she needed time, Blake decided, he had it. Suddenly, the idea of spending time in a cold, Australian winter instead of warm sunshine didn't seem so bad after all. He shrugged.

'What would you like to know?'

'Everything.'

'We only have twenty-five minutes left.'

'An abridged version is fine.'

'Fire away.'

'What was on the Greek island?' she asked, snuggling down into her chair and forcing herself to face him, annoyed by a deep curiosity.

'A holiday.'

'I'm sorry. This wasn't my idea,' she reminded him, feeling bad.

'Who needs the blue waters of the Aegean and sun-drenched beaches?' he shrugged, with an ironic grin.

'Are you a Victorian, too?'

He shook his head.

'I grew up in Sydney. My grandparents lived out west in the Blue Mountains. I spent most holidays with

17

them. They were great days and great people.'

Clare waited but when he didn't continue, she asked, 'Are your grandparents still alive?'

'No.'

His gaze refocused on her again.

'Besides being a farmer, my grandfather was a philosopher of sorts. We talked and argued and debated. I enjoyed it. When I finished high school, psychology seemed a natural progression.'

'Where do you practise?'

'Anywhere. Traumas, major disasters. I go where I'm needed.'

'Must be depressing.'

'On the contrary, it's highly rewarding.'

Clare hesitated.

'You seem unorthodox.'

If they were going to be honest with each other, they might as well start now. She preferred to know where she stood. Blake's mouth twitched in amusement. He finished his coffee and set down his mug.

'It's all about what makes people tick, learning the best way to approach and help them.'

His dark brown eyes roamed over her with steady intent.

'And when you're not working?'

Blake pushed back his shirt sleeve and consulted his watch.

'Fifteen minutes. Your turn.'

So much for Fielding's personal side. Well, it had been worth a try. Panic gripped Clare across the chest. She started to rise.

'Maybe tomorrow.'

Swiftly, Blake leaned forward and placed a firm hand on her arm.

'Maybe now,' he said gently, yet adamantly.

2

Clare realised she had reached a crossroad, a moment of decision, and the ramifications were frightening. She knew she must co-operate in order to move forward. But how did you open up to a total stranger, laying your innermost feelings bare?

She had discussed trial details with lawyers and police, but nothing personal. She had thought it would all go away and she would carry on as normal. That was her first mistake. The second was believing she could do it alone. Slowly, and only because of Blake's insistence, Clare sank back into her chair.

'This is a crazy idea.'

'It was Dan's,' he said gently. 'It's brilliant.'

His dark gaze threatened to strip away the protective shell she had built around herself for survival, leaving her exposed and vulnerable. Could she spill her hang-ups to this hunk of manhood? He didn't look like a shrink. In fact, he embodied every woman's romantic fantasy.

When she didn't respond, he prompted, 'I'm your friend, Clare.'

'Don't be presumptuous. We've only just met.'

'It's a place to start.'

'Start what?'

'The rest of your life.'

Clare gripped the sides of her chair, eyeing him warily.

'How much did Dan tell you?'

'Enough. Talk to me, Clare,' he urged softly.

'Where do I start?'

'At the beginning and work forward. What about your childhood?'

She raised surprised eyebrows and crinkled up her nose.

'I was all legs and scrawny,' she replied in total honesty.

'The cygnet who grew into a swan.'

'Flattery is good,' she quipped, to cover her pleasure and embarrassment at his compliment. 'I was painfully shy and 'way too conscientious. My dad had a small butchery in the neighbourhood, then supermarkets opened up and shopping habits changed so he sold up, mortgaged everything and moved into a shopping mall. His business boomed and my brother, David, is in partnership with him now.'

'Any other siblings?'

'One sister, Susan. She's a nurse in Hawaii. After the trial was over, I considered relocation there but I didn't want to endanger her life, too. You know I'm under witness protection and why?' she asked.

He nodded.

'According to the media, the trial's over, the case is closed and Anatole Guzzi is serving time.' Blake paused. 'You were his personal secretary?'

Clare nodded and her mouth twisted with irony.

'I soon learned staff was hand picked

for a reason. Apart from Toley, they didn't actually break the law. They just ensured deals went their way. Management and lawyers enjoyed outrageous perks, like luxury company cars and paid private education for their children. I was probably hired because I was green and they thought I could be manipulated.'

'And could you?'

A determined gleam entered her gaze.

'No. They exploited me but they never bought me. Anatole Guzzi operated a well-oiled machine of deception.'

'When did you begin to suspect him?'

'By the second year. Before that, I was a lap-dog loyal. I would never have believed a word against him. He was so smooth. By keeping my eyes and ears open, I accidentally stumbled across incriminating documents that were suspiciously false. I queried Toley and challenged why figures and dates didn't add up. All the evidence pointed to major fraud and corruption. It was a big company with big money and big names involved. I couldn't let it pass. The more I delved, the more suspect paperwork I found. I didn't like it and became afraid. Even so, I gathered up the nerve to confront him.'

'And what was his reaction?'

'At first he brushed it off. He just patted my head and spoke to me like a child, told me to stick to short skirts and flower arrangements. When I persisted, he bribed me but I refused all offers. That was the beginning of the end. From then on, every look and move he made held menace. He didn't fire me. Maybe he felt safer having me around. He could keep an eye on me. But I knew I had to inform on him. I couldn't let him escape justice.'

'What happened next?'

'I couldn't take it any higher in the company. I didn't know whom I could trust. So, I took my suspicions to the police and worked with them to gather more evidence. I went through every-thing, books, files, computers. It was obvious he was up to his handsome neck in fraud, diverting money from family companies to his own accounts, electronically.'

Clare shrugged.

'He had access to passwords and codes. Apparently those types of crimes are increasing and identifying cases can be difficult because of new technology and changes to banking practices. The police told me that sometimes even basic security isn't put in place and gaps are exploited. It was nerve wracking,' she admitted.

After a slight pause, she continued.

'I was a mess, terrified someone would walk in and catch me. The forged documents and extent of deception was unbelievable. Quite simply, Toley didn't believe the company was paying him enough. He was worth a fortune, and still wanted more. Toley was a powerful man with equally powerful friends. When he was finally arrested, he threatened me.'

Clare shivered, remembering.

'Phone calls, harassment. So they put me under witness protection and I've been anonymous ever since.'

'How did that make you feel?'

'Like a worm under a microscope. Defence lawyers tried to make me feel guilty as though I had committed the crime and not Toley. After it was over, they gave me a new identity and sent me here.'

Her mouth twisted in irony.

'With his silver tongue, Toley will talk his way out again in a few years.'

'Does that bother you?'

'What do you think?' she muttered, trying not to fidget.

'Are you going to let a criminal rule your life from prison?'

'He used me,' she said fiercely. 'You don't forget that overnight.'

'Sounds like you're too good for the Guzzi's of this world.'

Shocked by his openness, Clare murmured, 'In hindsight, I'm forced to agree. Strangely, I don't regret all of it. I got to travel. The trips were supposedly business but, in fact, were fabulous holidays. Mauritius, Tuscany, cruising on Toley's private yacht. Money was never a problem.'

'In time,' Blake assured her, 'you'll put Guzzi where he belongs, behind you. You'll be able to put him down to experience and move on. I gather he wasn't just your boss and he meant more to you than you ever did to him?'

Nobody had spoken to her with such blunt honesty since the whole mess flared up a year before and was publicly exposed. A lump rose in her throat and she fought it.

'Yes. I fell in love with him but he betrayed my trust. He's a highly-charismatic man,' she explained with regret. 'It hurts.'

'For now,' Blake said gently, 'and that's perfectly natural. But memories fade. If it's any consolation, everyone has a demon.'

Deftly, she tried to divert focus away

from her injured feelings.

'What's yours?'

Blake gave a soft chuckle.

'No, you don't. You still have five minutes left.'

Within thirty minutes, Clare felt she had established an alliance with this man but could she ever let him past her defensive wall to become a friend?

'Same time, same place tomorrow?' Blake asked over her thoughts.

'If I must.'

'You won't regret it.'

They rose together. Blake looked directly into her eyes and lightly placed his hands on her shoulders. She found his nearness unsettling.

'Clare, women, most of all, realise that the creation of life is a miracle. Don't you want to use the gift of life your mother gave you? I mean, really use it every day?'

'Sometimes,' she admitted in understatement.

'Only sometimes?' he quipped, resting the back of his hand beneath her chin, forcing her to look at him. 'Deep down, don't you want to scare the hell out of every minute you've got?'

She hesitated, stunned by the feel of his hands against her skin.

'I . . . guess.'

'But you're afraid to take the first step?'

'I don't even know what it is. If I did, I'd take it.'

'You already have. You're talking to me.'

'Not by choice.'

She looked vulnerable and helpless so he did something totally unprofessional and pulled her into his arms. He excused his action on the pretext that he doubted Clare had received any comfort in months. Just being held would be a form of security.

Clare allowed Blake's huge arms to wrap around her like a favourite, old blanket, his thick, sleeveless jacket soft against her cheek. One hand caressed her back, the other stroked her hair. She closed her eyes. Male or female, it had been for ever since she had experienced physical contact with anyone, and it felt so good.

For a moment, Blake lost himself in the feel of her, their shared warmth, her perfume, lightly flowered but not sweet. He'd have to control himself or they'd be in big trouble. He gave one final squeeze and released her.

'OK, let's think reward here, for having the courage to accept help and face me. Spoiled yourself lately?'

She thought for a moment.

'I phoned up for pizza three nights ago.'

Blake threw back his head and laughed.

'Given a choice, how would you really indulge yourself?'

'Ask me something easy,' she replied with a groan in her voice.

She realised this was probably part of his therapy and only fantasy so she gave her thoughts free rein. Heavens, she had forgotten how to have fun.

'It's been so long,' Clare confessed,

'but I'd love to just drain my mind. You know, chill out and think only beautiful, selfish, luxurious thoughts. Maybe wallow in a bubbling spa for an hour, or two, or a whole day, drinking champagne, eating chocolates.'

'Hold that thought,' was all he said, then he strode from the cabin.

During the day, the mist cleared and the sky turned blue. The mild air was perfect for venturing outdoors. She should do something, live, as Blake had urged. Instead, she played it safe. She washed their coffee mugs, straightened cushions and magazines, added wood to the fire then heated up a can of soup for lunch.

Restless, she prowled the house, watched the ferry's arrival and departure. Toward evening, Clare settled with a mystery novel that held her interest. How much more satisfying to have all the loose ends neatly tied up in fiction, she sighed, unlike real life. At sunset, long tree shadows stretched from the cabin to the lake's edge, the watery sun sinking in the west.

She heated another frozen dinner and watched the television news, feeling amazingly weary for such an inactive day. That night, for once, her body didn't put up its normal struggle to sleep. Ignoring the now familiar scuffling of nocturnal animals, Clare snuggled under the quilt, closed her eyes and slept.

Next morning she rolled over on to her back and put her hands behind her head, enjoying the best minutes of the day before she crept from between the warm covers. Today, she must become more active, maybe take a short walk. The idea daunted yet exhilarated her. She wondered when Blake would come over for his chat and coffee, reassured by the knowledge of an ally in her corner. After a hot shower, she pulled on a cream Aran sweater, black casual pants, thick socks and ankle-length boots. She wouldn't go far but was filled with a high sense of achievement at the thought of extending her self-imposed isolation.

She rekindled the open fire to warm the cabin. Then after breakfast, she stood at the window, scouring the bush to ensure no-one was about. Clare pulled on her parka and stepped outside warily. Winter mornings were pristine and magical, and she loved them. Why hadn't she done it sooner, and gone farther afield than the few steps down to the lake's edge?

White breath steamed around her as she ambled in the direction of the wharf. Then she retraced her steps for five minutes in the opposite direction. Feeling mildly smug and invigorated by her small accomplishment, she returned to the cabin.

Mid morning the telephone rang.

'Hi, it's me.'

Clare immediately recognised Blake's deep voice. She hadn't realised how welcome it would sound and how much emphasis she had unconsciously placed on hearing it again.

'Just warning you,' he said. 'Expect

visitors some time today.'

'You're not coming?'

She kicked herself for not disguising her disappointment.

'Sure. I promised, didn't I?'

Of course he had but she was programmed to doubt.

After a moment, Clare asked, 'So, who are these visitors?'

'Two big, strong men. It's a surprise.' He paused. 'You OK about it?'

Her heart warmed at this thoughtfulness. She sighed.

'Do I have a choice?'

'Nope. See you soon.'

To her frustration, he then hung up.

As promised, a truck and two men arrived before lunch. Clare peered out at them from behind the lace drapes. One of the men came to the door to verify her name and address. It was a test of her resilience and self-control not to slam the door in the workman's face and lock it, but she managed and realised afterwards the ordeal was not half as bad as she expected. One more step. She patted herself mentally on the back.

Remaining concealed, Clare watched the men open the rear of the truck, unloading hoses and piping, finally struggling with what looked like a huge, oval bath. Suddenly, it clicked. A spa! Blake had arranged her fantasy, here, at the cabin! What a charmer! She couldn't stop a smile spreading across her face as the workmen set it up on the porch, connected the motor and fittings then began to fill it with water. In childish excitement, Clare dashed into the bedroom and rummaged for a swimsuit and a warm robe.

When the tub was full, the workmen left. Already changed in anticipation, Clare stepped out on to the porch and was dipping her hands into the warm water, when Blake appeared, striding toward her wearing a black leisure suit and a broad grin. He clutched parcels hidden in green paper and tied with gold ribbon. When Clare accepted and excitedly unwrapped

35

them, she discovered a bottle of champagne and expensive chocolates.

'You remembered everything,' she said and laughed with pleasure.

Anxious to test the inviting spa waters, she wished Blake would leave, but even as the thought crossed her mind, he stripped down to a pair of black swim trunks.

'You're staying?'

'I'm game if you are.'

3

Impressed, Clare noted Blake's athletic and powerful body was in top shape. Maybe he worked out.

'Well, what are we waiting for?' he said. 'Let's not waste all this luxury.'

Feeling awkward and with a nervous grin, Clare shrugged off her robe. Without being too obvious, Blake skimmed his gaze over Clare as she disrobed. She was too thin. Poor appetite, he suspected. He steadied her elbow as she stepped into the spa and sank into the swirling water. She let out a pleasured moan and he chuckled, joining her on the opposite side. He then poured the champagne and raised his glass in a toast.

'To the rest of your life.'

'Amen to that.'

She took a sip. Covered to the

shoulders by the rolling water, Clare's mind eased. She let the water jets pummel her and the wine seep into her veins, the combination helping her unwind.

'Do you normally loosen tongues with champagne?'

'People talk if they're comfortable. Getting started can be a problem.'

He offered her a chocolate.

'Mmm, caramel,' Clare said as she bit into it. 'Try one.'

He did.

'Peppermint. You could get out more,' he hinted.

Back to reality already? Clare heaved a private sigh.

'Crowds terrify me, because of whom they might hide. Mr Dangerous.'

'Don't be too hard on yourself. You've made a start.'

'I think the phone might be tapped so I don't use it, and I don't send mail for fear of being traced.'

'What triggers your fear?'

'Suspicion.'

'And what happens when you're afraid?'

'I hibernate until the panic passes.'

'So, you end up alone? Must be death to your confidence.'

'Disastrous, yes.'

'Considering how dynamic you used to be, low self esteem must be quite a jolt.'

Yet again, Clare nodded grudgingly.

'Tried overcoming your fears?' he persisted.

'Yes, and failed. The mind is a powerful thing. It all seems too big and overwhelming.'

'Have your actions helped you so far?'

'Obviously not,' she said glumly.

'So these crises provoke irrational thoughts and behaviour, and cause you anxiety and depression, right?'

Clare nodded, remaining silent.

'What are the odds of you being found?'

'Slim, I guess,' she admitted.

'Do you think about the odds when you panic?'

'No. It consumes me and takes over all my thoughts and actions.'

'Do you see how this cycle of fear and negative results is stopping you from moving on?'

'Yes,' she admitted with quiet reluctance. 'But it's difficult when you're suddenly cut off from everything you have ever known. Your whole life and identity vanishes overnight, and I hated leaving my lovely terrace house in North Melbourne. I spent two years and every spare cent on renovations. Everything was sold and I received compensation. The proceeds are all in an untraceable account. Eventually I'll buy another home.'

She frowned and moved position in the bubbling water.

'But I'm worried about Sammy, my dog,' she said softly.

'Want me to follow it up?'

'That would be wonderful. Even though my family is within reach, I miss them all so much. I can contact them again. It should be safer now.'

Sensing her distress, Blake edged the conversation to happier ground.

'What's Sammy like?'

Clare needed no encouragement.

'He's a King Charles spaniel. A lovely cream and tan colour with huge eyes. He was the most affectionate companion.'

'Ideal for a career woman?' Blake suggested.

'More or less,' she admitted.

'Well, I guarantee you'll have plenty to keep you occupied from now on.'

Clare wasn't surprised to hear it. She was expecting action which, knowing Blake Fielding, would be sooner rather than later.

'Such as?' she queried.

'Desensitisation.'

She raised her eyebrows.

'Desensitising what exactly?'

'You. By monitoring your situation, relaxation and,' his voice lowered, accompanied by a wicked grin, 'by taking one little step at a time.'

Charmed, and because his light

41

mood was infectious, Clare flashed him an irresistible smile.

'Sounds promising. What's first?' she said, tilting her head to one side.

'Keep a record for a week. Identify and replace your irrational fears and behaviour.'

'What kind of record?'

'When you find yourself in a bad situation, ask if it's helping you. Challenge your reactions. If you feel someone is watching you, see if there's an alternative explanation or any evidence to support your anxiety. Is someone actually watching you, or do you just think they are? Take control of your fears,' he said firmly.

Then he showed her some intense deep-breathing exercises to practise for relaxation.

'Mmm, it really works,' Clare said later, eyes closed, head resting back against the spa, enjoying the warmth and massage of the water.

While she was still unwound and calm, he asked, 'How far can you go away from the cabin?'

She opened her eyes.

'Down to the lake. It's even stretching it being out here but you're with me and I feel safe.'

'Why?'

'Because I trust you.'

'When you're finished, you'll be able to trust everyone again.'

'Promises, promises,' she mocked in fun.

'Seriously. Starting with going farther, getting out to public places again.'

'Alone?'

Blake shrugged his broad, bare shoulders and held her gaze in challenge.

'Unless you want me along.'

'Of course I do!'

'At first, then you fly solo, OK?'

'Sure.'

But she wasn't.

'Each session when we talk again, you can tell me what you feel and how you dealt with it. In time, you won't let anything or anyone else control your life again. You'll find the strength inside yourself.'

'Sounds wonderful.'

Blake grinned and said pointedly, 'We'll take the ferry across to town.'

'Give me a decade for that. There must be thousands over there.'

Blake threw back his head and laughed, and Clare found herself transfixed by the deep, easy-going sound. She was amazed to discover she wanted to reach out to touch him. Instead, she sipped more champagne, sank lower into the relaxing bubbles and refocused her thoughts.

Feeling as if her burdens were now shared and her emotional load lighter, she suddenly realised how much time had flown. More than an hour, she was certain. She inspected her hands.

'We should get out of here. I'm looking like a prune.'

'You've done well today.'

He pushed himself from the water and extended her a hand. Clare grasped it and stood beside him, steadying

44

herself as she stepped out and reached for her robe. Blake retrieved his towel and rubbed himself down vigorously before donning his leisure suit again. Clare was mesmerised. He was an extremely handsome man.

'I've learned heaps today,' she confessed, tying her robe snugly against the cold. 'You've given me hope, a way through. Thank you. Talking to someone neutral is certainly different to testifying cold, hard facts in court.'

'Let's work on relegating Guzzi to your past where he belongs.'

'Definitely. He's wasted enough of my life.'

'Way to go, Clare. I'm proud of you. Thought about your future at all?'

'As a matter of fact, yes. Naturally I haven't done anything about it.'

'May I help?'

'Probably, but this is something I'll need to do myself, won't I?'

'Just testing. So, what are you planning?'

'I'd love to run my own business, a

marketing agency.'

'How do you plan to start?'

'Research. Ask around.'

'There's a need around here?'

She nodded, growing enthusiastic.

'There are a lot of craft people in the area. I'm considering some kind of co-operative, a centralised place where they could market their work. This is a huge tourist area. I'm positive the idea has potential.'

'Sounds like you're on your way. So, what's another special treat you would like as a reward for today's session?' he asked as they moved inside.

She thought about her life in isolation these past months, being alone, eating alone, and inspiration hit.

'A candlelit dinner, the works,' she said. 'I'm not much at cooking. I'd appreciate that. Coffee?' she called out as she moved into the kitchen.

He nodded.

'What would be on the menu?' he asked when she brought in their steaming mugs and settled into a chair.

'Steak, thick, medium rare, smothered in mushroom sauce, with a side salad, a smooth red wine, and to finish, a huge slice of the most decadent chocolate cake to be found, with short black coffee. Are you going to cook it for me?' she teased, grinning.

'I can barely boil water. You have expensive tastes.'

'Toley's influence maybe?'

'I'm sorry. I didn't mean to stir a memory.'

'It's all right,' she assured him. 'I'd be just as happy with fish and chips.'

'It gets easier,' he said gently.

Blake wanted to reach out and comfort her. He'd never had this problem with a client before. He was becoming far too involved. He refocused his thoughts. He admired Clare's efforts and progress. She had only needed a gentle nudge. It would take more time, of course, time he was more than prepared to give.

Clare regarded Blake with a level gaze.

'You enjoy doing this, don't you?'

'Absolutely. I get to help people, make a positive difference in their lives.'

His words made Clare realise the fragility of their connection. He would help her, leave and move on to heal someone else. For Clare, his presence meant much more. He was the first man she had befriended and trusted since Toley. If only for that, he was important in her life.

Before Blake left, she discovered that he had hired the spa for a week. Each subsequent time she used the revitalising indulgence, her thoughts inevitably returned to the one time she had shared it with Blake but she never fully recaptured the warmth and pleasure of that special day.

Every morning he came over for coffee. If the weather was too bleak or it rained, they stayed indoors. Other times, they walked farther around the lake foreshore, and always, Clare talked about Toley, their relationship, her crushed hopes and distorted life. The daily sessions, although brief, proved liberating. Her confidence grew and, with it, a reinstatement of her once familiar and higher self esteem.

'About Sammy, I have news,' he said one morning as they walked.

Clare stopped.

'Where is he?'

'With a good family, in the suburbs. Apparently he's thriving.'

She sent him a weak, grateful smile and rubbed her arms.

'Thanks. I was worried about him.'

They strolled on in silence, the tranquil beauty of the bush and lake a balm against past memories. Despite her fears of venturing farther away, the lure of time outdoors was a double-edged enticement, suspect but emotionally invigorating. Less and less, Clare cast dubious looks behind her at the increasing distance away from the cabin.

Yesterday, as they wandered toward the wharf, Blake had asked, 'Ever taken the ferry?'

Clare shot him a dark, long-suffering glance as though he hadn't absorbed anything she confided in recent weeks. He stopped and grinned.

'Worth a try. Too many people, huh? How about a bush hike then?'

'Better.'

'I'll come by about eight, OK?'

'So early?'

'It's a long walk. Think you're up to it?' he teased.

'I'll be right behind you every step of the way.'

Next morning, she dressed warmly in outdoor clothes. The day was cold and overcast, but calm. Blake appeared on time and they set off. On the lower reaches of the hillside, pink bell-shaped heather coloured the bush. Later, they encountered some grazing kangaroos, their grey-brown fur blending into the surroundings. Startled and wary, the powerful animals bounded away. She sympathised with their nervous flight, knowing exactly how they felt.

The hike was relatively peaceful and

only occasionally did they meet other bushwalkers. Within half an hour, the trail left the lakeside and climbed steadily alongside a stream. Soon, tree ferns crowded the gullies so thickly they could hear the gushing water but not see it. They walked in silence, their footsteps making dull thuds on the leafy trail, Blake a few steps ahead.

The therapeutic sounds of water and bird calls should have been calming, but Clare fought back a sudden attack of nerves and an irrational sense of being followed. More than once she spun around to see nothing but the empty path behind her and thick bush.

Get a grip, she told herself, to curb her overactive mind and pounding heart. Blake's with you. He's a big, strong man.

Later, she imagined noises again and froze.

'Blake!'

He stopped and turned.

'Did you hear anything?'

'No,' he answered.

'Are you sure?'

Noting her distress, he strode back toward her.

'Positive.'

'I could have sworn . . . ' she trailed off.

Blake gripped her shoulders.

'Did you see anyone?'

She shook her head.

'What are the chances of Toley being out here?' he asked, an ironic, loaded question since they both knew he was in prison.

'Slim,' she muttered sheepishly.

'Awareness and control, remember? That's all it takes. Would you rather walk ahead of me?'

'No. I'm sorry.'

'You're safe. There's no-one here but me. Try some of that deep, steady breathing I showed you.'

She did and within minutes her panic abated and they continued. From time to time they stopped to catch their breath, take photographs or simply sit on a rock to appreciate the view.

By late morning, their ascent brought them to the top of the hill with a stunning view over the lake and village below.

'Worth it, huh?' Blake said and flashed her an entrancing smile that stole her breath away.

'Absolutely.'

To take her mind off his presence, she slid off her backpack and removed her parka. She gnawed her bottom lip as she searched for her water bottle. It was always the wrong man or the wrong time. Dan Fielding had made it quite plain he was out of bounds, but he was right. Despite his strong attraction, the thought of unlocking her heart again so soon was madness. Resisting all men was imperative until she felt emotionally stronger and had fully accomplished starting again.

She moved to the edge of the hilltop, surveying the magical scenery below. She jumped when Blake appeared beside her and their shoulders brushed. Although he must have felt it, he made no comment on her tension. He just stood quietly alongside and absorbed the mind-healing view.

'You're quite an outdoor person, aren't you?' Clare said eventually.

He shrugged.

'My grandparents lived in the Blue Mountains. Climbing and hiking are in my blood. You'll find it beneficial, too. You'll recover more completely if you do it physically and emotionally.'

'In my other life, I never found much time for leisure.'

'Solitude's good for the soul and inner peace,' Blake said quietly. 'Now, you've exercised your body, now let's feed it.'

He edged a space with stones and rocks, then built a fire and handed her a blackened billy from his rucksack.

'Fetch us some water from the stream to boil for lunch.'

She did so and he set it over the flames. Clare munched ravenously on her sandwich, then unwrapped some fruit cake and offered Blake a slice.

After lunch, a chill breeze swept up through the bush from below and she shivered. Blake eyed her closely.

'Put on your coat and come closer to the fire.'

Dubious, Clare complied and sat next to him, having kept her distance for a reason. He hooked the boiling billy can away from the coals with a stick and set it on the ground, throwing in a handful of tea. While it steeped, he produced a bag of marshmallows from his pack.

Clare scoffed.

'You told me only to pack essentials.'

'Marshmallows are exempt.'

Piercing one on the end of a twig, Blake twirled it over the embers until it was brown and melting. When he leaned closer and offered it to her, their boots and knees touched. Clare couldn't get it off the twig and giggled, her fingers sticky. Their eyes met and she was drawn into an enticing unknown. Blake's voice grew husky.

'Right about now, I wish . . . '

'Don't,' she whispered, interrupting him deliberately.

He pulled his mouth into a grim line of regret then turned away and gazed out over the treetops.

'Don't lock yourself away when the time comes, Clare. You're destined to settle down some day. You're a nester. You need a stable man and kids.'

His pronouncement was a jolt, seriously close to reality. Once, her career had been everything but Clare realised ambition was no longer important.

'Don't be afraid to let someone else into your heart eventually,' he said. 'Ever heard the saying, love as though you have never been hurt before?'

Clare shook her head. Promising words to remember that identified the depth of trust and faith needed to give your heart away. She liked it.

'I'm taking one day at a time, as you suggested,' she pointed out.

One day, she thought, she might take a chance, but not yet.

Later, they packed up, doused the campfire and began their descent to the lake. More relaxed now, Clare took some photographs as they followed the trail and were soon back where they started near the cabins.

Clare knew she should have felt content after their hike, stimulated by Blake's company and pleasantly weary after outdoor activity. Instead, a ball of frustration knotted her stomach.

'Want to come in for a coffee?' she asked.

'It's getting late.'

'Please yourself,' she responded coolly. Her voice was unsteady.

'I thought you enjoyed our day,' he said gently.

She liked that, our day.

'I did.'

'Then what's the matter?'

'Nothing. I'm just tired.'

'Chicken,' he teased.

'Hardly. I've purged my soul to you for weeks now.'

'That's not what I meant and you

know it. You're mad because we have to back off.'

She didn't answer but he read the stricken truth on her face.

'Clare, we must. This is work. I thought you understood,' he said.

Clare sighed. Meeting him and being attracted was rotten timing. She knew that. How could she have forgotten?

'Sure. Thanks for today,' she muttered ungraciously, unlocking her door.

'See you tomorrow.'

Some consolation, she guessed, and nodded.

Inside, Clare closed the door and leaned back against it. She had just made the biggest fool of herself. The day Blake arrived, she had offered him a cup of coffee and thirty minutes of her time. Now she couldn't see enough of him, against all commonsense.

From Clare's cabin, Blake stalked through the bush to his own. She had feelings for him, big time, and he felt more than protective toward her in return, feelings, for her sake, he must conceal. Heaven knows, she was a beautiful woman and he had slipped a few times, giving her the wrong idea.

The solution, of course, was not to see her at all but they weren't finished with her sessions. No way would he leave her now and jeopardise her full recovery. Until then, he couldn't admit or pursue the chemistry he felt.

Monday morning, Blake and Clare were extra polite with each other. Somehow Clare managed to focus. Blake stayed an hour then left. In between, she moped, frustrated by his necessary detachment. She dreaded the week's end because she had foolishly promised to try the ferry. The thought of all those people jammed around her was appalling and she slept restlessly. Annoyed by her lack of control, she pushed herself to address the forthcoming situation rationally and without panic, as Blake had counselled.

He had tried to make it easier for her.

'We'll sit in a quiet corner, OK?' he said one morning after a walk.

'Quiet? On that boat?' she had disagreed, hands clenched by her sides.

'Then we'll take it off-peak,' he suggested. 'I'll meet you down there.'

'You're not coming to get me?'

His dark eyes dared her to be strong.

'The wharf, tomorrow, eleven-thirty sharp.'

She scowled at the ground as she returned to her cabin. You can do this, she told herself. Where's that dynamic woman who thrived on city life? A few people on a ferry should be a snap.

4

Getting ready the next morning, Clare fussed with her appearance, convincing herself it was pride, nothing more, and she didn't really care what Blake thought. She chose a long tartan skirt, a black lambswool jumper and black boots, bundling up her hair into a manageable fall with wide combs. She threw a coat and scarf over her arm and headed off.

Nearing the ferry wharf, her steps slowed. She concentrated on deep breathing and scanned the small, waiting crowd. There was no sign of Blake or anyone else she recognised.

After fifteen interminable minutes of pacing and uncertainty, he still hadn't arrived. She forced herself to be realistic and face people. Everyone looked harmless enough. There was a mother with three children, one in a stroller, the other two scampering about; an elderly couple together, holding hands; individuals travelling alone. Gradually, they all boarded. Alone on the wharf, Clare grew edgy.

Blake studied Clare through his binoculars from a safe distance back among the trees. She was restless, checking her watch too often. She hadn't bought tickets yet and was making no move to board alone. But, to her credit, she had toughed it out and stayed. She sure looked good in a skirt. Whatever she had done to her hair, he liked it. He pocketed his travel binoculars and sauntered down to meet her.

Clare's palms were damp despite the cold. Where was Blake? She had considered buying tickets but no way would she get on that boat without him. Then he came into view. His coat collar was pulled up and, in her immense relief, she thought him the most welcome sight she had ever seen. Her heart skipped a beat and annoyance surfaced at her insecurity.

'Where have you been?' she demanded, her eyes alive and stormy.

'Missed me, huh? Bought our tickets?'

'Of course not,' she retorted. 'I didn't think you were going to make it.'

'If I hadn't, would you have gone alone?'

Something about his soft dare behind the question and his mischievous gaze made Clare suspicious. Reality hit.

'You deliberately kept me waiting!'

Furious, and not waiting for confirmation, Clare turned her back on him and bought a single ticket. Let him buy his own. Right now, she didn't care if he came with her or not. She just needed to escape and collect her wits. How dare he abandon her like that! She should have found comfort knowing he had watched out for her but resentment built at his stealth, even if well-meant. She found an empty bench inside the ferry and sat by a window, staring out blindly at the watery blue sky and grey-green water. Anger distracted her nerves. She could ride the ferry across and back, sit tight and endure the journey then return to the security of her cabin.

Blake joined her, leaving a space between them like neutral ground. He stretched a hand across the back of the seat as the ferry engine rumbled into life and the vessel left the wharf for the short lake crossing.

'It was a test,' he said finally.

'I failed,' she muttered.

He covered her cold hands with his big warm ones and shook his head.

'Wrong. You didn't leave. You stuck it out. Next time, it will be a breeze.'

Warmed by his support, she said, 'You're just telling me that to make me feel better.'

'No. You've started to meet people halfway.'

In an unexpected and tender gesture, he brushed stray, wind-blown curls from her cheek.

When the ferry docked, they waited until last to disembark.

'You OK?' Blake asked and as Clare shook her head, he noticed she wiped a sweaty palm down the side of her skirt.

'There's a big difference between a group of ferry passengers and facing an entire town,' she said nervously.

'I'm here.'

He stood up and held out his hand. She clutched it and rose beside him, his warm fingers firmly wrapped around hers. Encouraged, she moved forward and stepped on to the wharf at the bottom end of the town's main street. She scanned the unfamiliar surroundings, just to be sure, then looked across at Blake. The fresh wind off the water played with his tousled hair.

Blake privately cursed her soft red lips begging to be kissed. Pulling out all the stops on his self control, he compromised and kissed her on the cheek instead, proud of his restraint.

Startled, Clare asked, 'What was that for?'

'Achievement,' he winked. 'Let's do lunch.'

He held out his arm and she linked hers into it as they headed along the main street.

'Look everyone in the face, and smile,' he urged. 'They'll be so busy looking at a gorgeous woman, you'll take their mind off everything else.'

Gorgeous? A curl of pleasure rolled through her stomach. It took determination but Clare took his advice, flattered when it resulted in second glances from men.

'I only said smile,' Blake whispered.

'That's what I'm doing.'

'You're flirting,' he accused, sounding disapproving.

'I'm just being friendly.' Feeling mischievous, she caught his gaze and quipped, 'Jealous?'

'I'm not a rival for your heart,' he drawled, casting her a steady gaze.

His warning shouldn't have stung but it did. Back off, he was saying. This is strictly business. And Clare knew he was right.

'This do for lunch?' he asked,

pausing by an outdoor café.

Clare nodded and Blake led her to a seat in a far corner, away from others. Blake leaned back in his chair, put his hands behind his head and closed his eyes, soaking up the sun.

'This could almost be the Mediterranean,' he murmured.

Clare immediately felt guilty.

'This should be the Mediterranean.'

His eyes flickered open.

'My choice,' he assured her softly.

He would never tell her he flipped a coin with Mac and considered he'd lost, until they met.

Clare sighed and resigned herself to the long haul of readjustment. With concentration, she lessened her mistrust of others and actually enjoyed lunch. They ordered fish freshly caught that morning from the lake, served with a Caesar salad and chilled white wine.

Later, lazy from sunshine and wine, they walked off their meal. Clare's gaze still flickered in every direction, although with less concern. She grew more observant than watchful as she strolled alongside Blake.

On her arrival in town over a month ago, she had driven right past the quaint main street. Barely aware of it, she had hurtled past in her vehicle along the bypass road, intent on finding her secluded cabin in the bush and retreating from the world.

Today, Clare noted that most of the original buildings remained, giving the entire street a timeless charm. Understandable that the township was a weekend mecca for tourists and day trippers lured from the city by the unique setting and tranquil bush. Shops, cafés, restaurants, antique shops, galleries, all had been renovated or well-maintained with lacework verandas. The township obviously supported a thriving art community and Clare was excited to have the need for her business confirmed.

Blake paused in front of an ice-cream kiosk.

'My treat. What flavour?'

'Double chocolate chip.'

'I should have guessed, if you love chocolate cake.'

He hadn't forgotten. Maybe she would get that dinner after all. Blake chose rum and raisin, and they continued their leisurely exploration. Only two shops were vacant in the main street. Clare itched to enquire about rental but, although she had coped with today's outing, she felt daunted by any thought of the next large stride, to begin organising her new venture.

A broad, landscaped park with gardens and winding pathways stretched down to the edge of the lake, and they sauntered along it back to the ferry. Passing swings in a children's play area, Blake stopped.

'Hop on. I'll give you a push.'

'No! I couldn't. I'd look ridiculous.'

'Five or fifty, I doubt you'll ever manage that.'

He took her coat and bag and tossed them on the ground.

'Come on. Kids shouldn't have all the fun.'

Clare rolled her eyes in despair, sensing it was useless to argue, and settled on to the seat. She gave herself a short kick and started swinging. Blake pushed her higher.

'That's enough,' she protested, laughing, loose strands of her upswept hair swirling around her face and shoulders as she swung, her expression rapt from the simple pleasure.

For the first time in weeks, Clare's face glowed, revealing the real woman hidden beneath a cloud of unwanted memories.

'We used to have a swing under a giant, old tree in our backyard,' she called out in mid-air. 'I spent hours on the thing, just swinging like this.'

Blake plucked a blade of grass and chewed on it. After a while, Clare jumped off and hurtled across the grass, her face alive with happiness. He caught her before she stumbled. Holding her steady, Clare was irresistibly magnetic. For a moment, Blake's eyes focused on her lips and his mind wandered on to dangerous ground. He clenched his jaw against the temptation to overstep the barrier between counsellor and client.

He indulged his gaze a moment longer, then removed his hands from her body as if he had been burned. Forcing a coolness he didn't feel, he scooped Clare's coat and bag off the ground.

'Need more groceries?' he asked.

Confused by his sudden change of mood and sensing they had shared a fleeting connection of phenomenal importance, Clare gave an unwilling nod.

'Then let's hit the general store. How did you manage before?'

'Telephoned them with an order for home delivery and made them leave the groceries outside on the veranda,' she confessed, recalling the courage she needed each week just to call.

Inside the store, Blake pushed the

shopping trolley around the aisles, trailing Clare as she selected. The noise and bustle of the busy store caused an unwanted but familiar surge of panic. Suddenly jumpy and watchful again, she hurried her shopping so they could leave. At the checkout, the cashier greeted them warmly. She chatted as she scanned their order.

'Haven't seen you around,' she addressed Clare. 'Staying long?'

She took a deep breath before she could answer.

'Yes. I've just moved here to live.'

'You'll love it,' the girl assured her, beaming. 'The township has a great community spirit.'

Clare was pleased to hear it and planned to participate when she mustered more courage. Since credit cards were traceable, she paid for her groceries in cash and Blake carried them back to the ferry. Annoyed with her lapse in the store, which she believed she had controlled sufficiently to pass Blake's notice, Clare vowed to be more positive in future. By the time they neared the wharf, she was composed again.

Because they approached the ferry from the opposite direction this time, Clare noticed a church through the trees on the lake's edge that wasn't visible earlier. For some reason, it intrigued her and she was seized by an impulse to investigate. Passengers were boarding but there was still time.

Pointing in the direction of the half-hidden building, she said, 'Just going to take a look.'

Blake raised his eyebrows.

'Want me to come?'

'No, I'll be fine,' she said with confidence and meant it.

Adrenalin pumped through her as she followed a gravelled pathway to the small white timber building. Its simple gardens were beautifully kept, its arched, stained-glass windows brilliant in the afternoon sun. As a church should be, it was open. Inside was hushed.

She sat in a pew, enthralled by the huge picture window above the altar through which worshippers had an uninterrupted view across the lake. She marvelled how anyone concentrated on the service with such a stunning view to distract them. Feeling peaceful and calm, she rose to leave.

Clare suffered a moment of anxiety as she searched the crowd inside the packed ferry for Blake, until she caught his wave.

'That's the first time you've gone off alone voluntarily,' he murmured as she sat beside him.

The engines started and the ferry moved off.

'Yes, it is,' she beamed.

Blake knew she had reached a milestone today. She would still experience uncertainty but was well on the way to recovery. The knowledge wrenched him with bitter sweetness for it heralded the beginning of the end.

As they left the ferry and walked toward the cabins in silence, the trees made long shadows across the grass. Blake dumped Clare's groceries in her kitchen. Looking awkward for no particular reason, he hovered in the centre of the room. Today, in the most subtle way, their relationship had deepened, taking them far beyond friendship. With difficulty, Clare kept her feelings hidden. From his actions, Blake clearly felt the same and fought it, but she knew professionalism restrained him.

Lost, she unpacked the groceries. Suddenly, Blake strode for the door, turning before he left.

'You did great today.'

'Thanks.'

'See you tomorrow.'

There seemed nothing more to say so she merely nodded, wishing they had met at another time and in another place, under completely different cir-cumstances. The front door closed and through the window, she watched him take the steps two at a time and stride off down the driveway. He seemed eager to escape, run away, ignore the truth, as they must.

In the following days, Blake remained casual and reserved but Clare always anticipated his arrival, not only for his treasured company, but their talks. Their final sessions changed. One hour became two. One cup of coffee became three. In a positive development, Clare finally accepted Toley's deception and place in her past. Forgiveness gave her freedom to disassociate herself from him and move on.

Seated on the sofa, his long legs stretched out into the room, Blake said, 'You've dealt with Guzzi and feel secure. But what about when he's eventually paroled? How will you feel about that?'

Clare roamed her living-room. Often, she found it difficult to sit calmly and chat, not only because of Blake's unsettling presence but because of warmer, sunny days and a bursting of renewed life and energy within her. She paused in her wanderings and leaned against the mantelpiece.

'You mean he might try to contact me?'

Blake nodded.

'In ten years' time? I doubt he'll bother. If and when it ever happens, I'll deal with it then,' she said. 'And he'd have to find me first, wouldn't he?'

'You know you can call me any time to talk, even after I've left.'

It would happen soon. He hadn't said exactly when but it was his tactful way of preparing the path to separation. She tried to be mature and strong.

'Thank you. I'll keep that in mind.'

Clare's only regret in recent weeks was that she had talked exclusively about herself and learned little about Blake. Whenever she tried, he had cleverly diverted the conversation.

As the weeks slid by, so did the season. Late winter quietly eased itself upon the landscape with prolonged sunny outbursts, promising spring.

'How about we hire a canoe on Sunday?' Blake said one Friday.

That would certainly bring them into close proximity, Clare mused, and test their resilience, surprised he would suggest it.

'Sure,' she agreed.

Accordingly, Saturday dragged. To keep occupied, Clare actually did housework under the guise that she would be vacating the cabin soon and must clean it anyway. Then she heated another boring microwave dinner and took an extra long walk along the lake. She also did something she hadn't done since she arrived. She opened the garage door on her small car. Dusty and neglected, she washed it and vacuumed the interior. The motor kicked over and, on such a magnificent day, Clare was tempted to take a spin but didn't. The preparation was enough. Soon she would take a spin.

Sunday dawned perfect. After lunch, she pulled on an oatmeal sweater over black cord jeans, let her hair swing free and walked down to the wharf to meet Blake. This time, she noted with a private smile, he was already there, waiting. She guessed it was a positive omen. These days, he didn't need to hide and she harboured few qualms.

He lounged against one wall of the hire boat shed, his legs and arms crossed. Clare stopped mid-stride and stared at him. When they parted, this would be the vision she wanted to remember.

'I've already arranged a boat,' he said and took her arm. 'Let's go.'

Not surprisingly, the sunny weekend had drawn locals and weekenders to launch every type of boat out on to the lake. Masts pierced the air and colourful sails billowed in the light wind. They scrambled into the canoe, donned life jackets and Blake rowed them away from the shore. Later, it was Clare's turn. Under her control, the oars splashed awkwardly in the water, but at least they moved. Blake sat back, hands behind his head, grinning with amusement at her clumsy but determined efforts.

Eventually, lazy, they secured the oars and drifted. They didn't talk much, just watched other boats. With both their legs outstretched, their sneakers touched in the centre of the boat and she clamped down on a deep well of regret. They could share so much, if only . . .

Blake gathered in the oars and rowed them ashore. He jumped out first, pulled the boat up on to a crescent of sand and helped Clare alight. His hands settled over her slim waist beneath the sweater and she gripped his arms for support. The moment passed in the swiftness of a heartbeat but lasted long enough to send sparks to every nerve ending Clare possessed.

She held her breath. For that suspended moment of time, Blake didn't say or do anything and his face was unreadable. Whatever his feelings, he shuttered them. Then they stepped apart and it was business as usual. They removed their bulky life jackets and sat on them.

'So, what are your intentions about your business?' he asked, breaking the silence.

Clare hugged her knees. The light breeze tugged at her hair.

'I've been planning in my head and on paper. I need to make enquiries and speak to people. I intend renting a shop.'

'You're definitely staying then?'

'Yes.'

Anywhere peaceful was fine. She wanted to decrease the speed of her life. Here was as good as anywhere.

'I've come to appreciate stress-free, country life.'

'Fair enough.'

His reply was guarded. He could at least have shown some enthusiasm. He was usually supportive.

'When do you want to start?'

'As soon as possible.'

'Tomorrow?'

'I guess so.'

'We'll skip our session then?'

Clare swallowed and managed a smile.

'I guess so. I have heaps to do.'

'Great. Let me know when you want to meet again.'

His easy tone suggested her independence didn't bother him at all. He wouldn't miss her.

'Good luck,' was all he said when they parted later.

Next morning, Clare was too nervous for breakfast, nervous about going it alone yet knowing she must. She felt overwhelmed by insecurity and longed to phone Blake. Instead, she drank two cups of strong coffee, slowly, and then dressed carefully in a snappy beige suit, pinched in at the waist, a darker silk shirt, gold jewellery and black heels. The outfit felt strange after wearing casual clothes for months. The mirror told her she presented a professional image. Inside, a bunch of knots sat in her stomach.

She gathered up her notes, and stuffed them into a briefcase. She was as ready as she would ever be, for business, for action, for the rest of her life. She wanted Blake to see her, check with him, be reassured, but dared not. This was another step and she must take it alone, without Blake, for herself.

She made some telephone calls then strode out to the garage. As before, the car started first try, the weather held and the sun shone. Good omens, she decided, as she drove into town, growing excited instead of afraid to be in control of her life again. It was scary and thrilling to be out alone, but something was missing — being with Blake. It was definitely more fun doing things with another person.

In town, she parked behind the main street shops and kept her first appointment for the day. The real estate agent, Mr Palmer, middle-aged and distinguished, accompanied her along the street to inspect the two vacant shops. Clare explained her proposed business and her needs, investigated each building carefully, and finally chose the larger premises.

She stipulated the repairs she wanted

and the charming man even reduced her rent for the first six months. Clare suspected he was just relieved to lease the property.

She took a cappuccino break at the outdoor café where she and Blake had eaten on her first visit to town, then searched for office furniture. She discovered an unassuming shop crammed with second-hand goods and old wares. Browsing found her all the pieces she needed to give her office character at bargain prices and she arranged to have them held until the shop was ready.

By mid afternoon, Clare was exhausted and called it a day. She drafted an advertisement for staff, lodged it with the local newspaper, then stopped at the post office to rent a mailbox and collect any mail, not that she expected any but to her delight, Mary had written. Recently, shelving aside another small barrier, Clare had finally put pen to paper. In a stubborn streak of defiance, she had written to

Dan's wife who had become a good friend during the trial, revealing her location and ignoring any possible unwanted consequences. The rebellious gesture was stimulating and Clare wondered why she hadn't done it sooner.

In the parked car, Clare ripped open Mary's letter and eagerly read the newsy, four-page contents. She had even enclosed drawings from Josh, the youngest of their three sons, scratchy pieces of nonsense but Clare loved every indecipherable line. Excited to have overcome another milestone, she sped to Blake's cabin to share her news. The instant she turned into his driveway and saw two vehicles instead of one, she felt like a trespasser. He had a visitor.

Clare left her car idling, tempted to reverse and go home, unwilling to intrude, when Blake and a young woman appeared from indoors. He beckoned, so Clare cut the engine, got out and walked to greet them. She breathed a sigh of relief that she was well-dressed, for the young woman at his side was tall and reed-slim. Her glossy brunette hair, cut short, outlined an elfin face. Her long legs stretched out for ever beneath a scandalously short mini skirt, held up with matching braces over a soft white sweater.

'Clare, this is my secretary, April Charles.'

The girl extended a hand and smiled.

'Call me Charlie. Everyone does.'

She looked up at Blake with a doting gaze, laid a familiar hand on his sleeve and kissed him on the cheek.

'See you soon.'

Clare was seized by a flash of jealousy.

After Charlie left, Blake eyed Clare with an appreciative gaze.

'You look fabulous. Coming inside?'

Her heart raced.

'No, I won't stay.'

Suddenly her impulsive decision and reason to call seemed childish.

'Have a good day?'

'Wonderful,' she replied with a quick laugh, more at ease. 'I did too much and loved every minute of it.'

'No problems?'

He raised his eyebrows, watchful of her reaction. There was a mountain of meaning behind his words. Clare shook her head.

'Congratulations.'

He nodded to her envelope.

'Good news?'

'Oh, yes, a letter from Mary. It's nothing really, just a small thing. It seemed important . . . '

She trailed off, aware she was babbling. His warm smile encouraged her so she continued.

'I wrote, actually posted a letter in the mail, and she replied. It was so good to hear from her. Of course, I should have contacted her sooner as you suggested. Thanks,' she ended, shuffling with discomfort.

She had walked miles today and her feet ached. He inclined his head.

'I'm always here for you.'

He was staring at her in a deliciously odd way.

'It was foolish of me, I know, but I just wanted to let you know.'

'Pleased you did. As it happens, I have something to tell you, too.'

His words held an ominous ring.

'Sit down.'

He patted the top step and they perched on it together. Clare took comfort in the warmth of his fingers wrapped around hers when he sought them. She removed her high heels and rubbed her feet.

'Charlie drove up here because an urgent job has arisen, an accident on a construction site in Darwin. Most of the men will need counselling. I'll be away for a week.'

'Oh.'

It was all she could manage. She could hardly throw her arms around his neck and beg him to stay. He didn't belong to her. She had no rights where Blake was concerned, no rights at all.

'Leaving Wednesday,' he whispered.

Today was Monday. Seven days. How would she survive? Clare forced a cheerful smile.

'You're coming back?' she asked lightly.

'To say goodbye.'

She went numb at his words. The notion hit her that she was on borrowed time and her biggest test was yet to come — letting Blake go. At least he wasn't leaving permanently, yet. This time would be a practice run, she told herself wryly. The reality was, they must part. Blake had a job to do, places to go. Clare's new life awaited. She was under no illusion that their parting would be easy. She replaced her shoes and stood up.

'Will I see you tomorrow?'

She hoped her casual tone fooled him.

Blake rose beside her.

'Afraid not. I leave before daylight Wednesday morning. Charlie's booked me on an early flight. She knows where to reach me.'

Again, Clare found herself envious of Blake's young secretary, privy to all those personal details he withheld from her, apparently unable or unwilling to share. He hesitated and she drowned in his deep gaze.

'I promise I'll come and see you first thing Monday when I get back.'

She was about to descend the steps when he reached out and caught her arm, bending forward to kiss her on the lips, the best and worst thing he could have done. Clare's body became a furnace of reaction as an explosion of molten heat burned its way from her mouth down through her body. Blake broke away, his eyes conveying an equally confused message.

'See you next week.'

'Yes,' she breathed, thinking it might as well be for ever.

Still bewildered from his blistering kiss, Clare turned on her heel and left. She was proud of her carefree smile and wave, for they concealed a wealth of misery.

Blake watched Clare leave. Her lips had just betrayed her and he wondered how their friendship would be resolved. He stood on the veranda staring after her until her vehicle was out of sight. He had been around, worked and played hard all his life, shunning involvement, until a gorgeous brunette had exploded on to the scene, blasting away all of his bachelor dogmas and habits. One thing he knew for sure. The second hardest thing he would ever do would be to leave the woman he had just kissed goodbye. The hardest would be leaving her for a whole week.

Clare would manage without him. She was a survivor and stronger than she thought. She would cope. It wouldn't be easy but she would make it. Question was, how would he manage without her? For a grown man who prided himself on remaining impervious to emotions and long-term commitment, the truth staggered him.

It was hard to back off.

5

Next morning, Clare phoned a young builder, Steve Wagner, listed in a local trade directory. After an initial consultation and estimate, he began work on her shop renovations.

That evening, she took home Asian food, to avoid cooking. She only picked at it and stored the leftovers in the refrigerator. Preoccupied with Blake's imminent absence, she undressed, stood under a long, hot shower, then crawled despondently into bed.

After a sleepless night, she woke to the knowledge that Blake would be gone, flying at thirty thousand feet heading for the Northern Territory. Having seen him daily for weeks, being without him was a radical change. She couldn't dismiss her feelings for him but she could stop moping that he was away with little possibility that they would ever end up together. Fortunately, building a new routine was therapy in itself.

In her new office in town, she worked around Steve's noise and sawdust as best she could. The telephone buzzed constantly in response to her advertisement for staff so she noted names and set up appointments for the following week. Before returning to the cabin, she checked her mailbox then drove home to deal with it.

Around midnight, Clare clicked out the lights and headed for bed. She had barely fallen into a doze, when she heard scuffling sounds outside. She moaned and pulled the quilt over her ears. Didn't possums ever sleep? Then she heard it again, louder, rustling alongside the cabin wall. She frowned. Didn't possums mostly stick to trees? Alarmed, she sat bolt upright, clutching the quilt around her.

Fully awake, she tensed, listening. Motionless, she waited for at least five minutes, but didn't hear anything else.

She dismissed her fears and practised controlled breathing until her heartbeat slowed. Impatient with herself for being unnecessarily suspicious, she flopped back down on to the pillow and, much later, eventually fell asleep.

All the same, for peace of mind in the morning Clare went outside to investigate. Beneath her bedroom window she discovered broken branches on shrubs and fresh, deep footprints in soft soil close to the cabin wall. She decided not to panic and rejected phoning Dan or the local police, simply resolving to stay alert.

For the rest of the day, tension from interrupted sleep and the unsettling knowledge of a possible prowler made Clare edgy. When Steve asked her something she had previously explained, her patience snapped.

'Steve, you know what I want. I've drafted a plan for you to follow which we discussed in detail yesterday. I thought you were experienced.'

Undaunted by her outburst, he

shrugged and grinned.

'Just double checking. You've changed your mind about it once already.'

She inhaled deeply and sighed.

'Yes, I have. Steve, I apologise.'

'Pressure of setting up a new business, eh?'

'You're probably right. I'll try and do better.'

She could hardly confess to being paranoid about phantom night noises, nor a desperate longing for a man she had no logical reason or right to let into her heart. But when was falling in love ever logical?

'Haven't forgotten our dinner invitation?' Steve reminded her later.

'Heavens, no. A meal I don't have to cook?' She laughed. 'I'm there.'

During conversation and coffee breaks, Clare discovered Steve and his wife, Karen, were her neighbours not much farther around the lake. She had begun to experience the reassurance of familiar faces around town even after only a few days of open circulation among them. Some were already potential friends which lessened her loneliness since being wrenched away from her former life and plunged into a new one.

The week proved hectic which helped Clare cover her sense of loss in Blake's absence. The sun rose. She worked hard. The sun set. Coupled with her anxiety over the continuing nocturnal noises, she felt desolate and exhausted. For extra security, she kept the cordless telephone in her bedroom at night. Nothing had happened. No crime had been committed. It occurred to her that Toley could be behind all this but, using Blake's suggested rationalisation techniques, she dismissed it. All the same, she kept all windows and doors locked.

By the week's end, her office alterations were complete, the painters applied the finishing touches and the telephone was connected. She wanted everything perfect for Blake's return.

Driving back to the cabin Friday

night, Clare acknowledged that Blake could be with another woman and she wouldn't know. Although under no illusion that their friendship was even remotely serious, albeit holding immense potential if they both dropped their guard, Clare shrank from the thought. Blake was a vibrant, attractive man. Despite fighting them, her feelings had grown and turned to love. It might make the world go around but it could also make a person's life extremely miserable.

Having Saturday and Sunday free was bliss but also a mistake. Free and relatively unoccupied, Clare dwelt on Blake's return. What would it mean? Had he missed her? She lost sleep and by Monday morning was an emotional wreck. She rose early and indulged in a long bath. Wrapped in her white robe, hair wild, she selected and discarded half a dozen outfits for Blake's arrival.

Finally choosing one, she waited at home, afraid to go into the office in case she missed him. The hours ticked by. Still Blake didn't appear, which was unlike him. Normally a morning person, he had promised to come over first thing and Clare trusted his word, so far unbroken.

Close to midday, Blake finally ambled along her driveway. The refreshing sight of the man she loved was like a reviving charge of electricity to her body and Clare realised she had been emotionally dead for six days. How she wanted and needed him, and wished she didn't. Why did he have to be so handsome? So sensitive and understanding? Considerate and perceptive to her needs? All the things Toley had never been.

Clare noticed his normally confident stride was sluggish, and as he reached the veranda, he looked tired. Her heart went out to him. It must have been a tough week. The shadows on his face dissolved when they met, and they grinned at each other. He stood in the doorway, hands sunk into the pockets of his navy cord slacks.

Blake knew he had been wrong the moment he set eyes on Clare again. The hardest part hadn't been leaving her. It was coming back and trying to keep his hands off. He hadn't realised how much he missed her and closed the door behind him. She was a knockout and no mistake. Her hair spilled freely around her face and over her shoulders. The top half of her body, as shapely as he remembered, was seductively packaged in something silky, nipped into the waist of a tight black skirt. His gaze slithered down the shapely legs to her stockinged feet. He stepped closer.

' 'Morning.'

'I missed you,' she said without thinking.

Blake's jaw clenched.

'I wish you hadn't.'

'I mean our sessions,' she corrected, clasping her hands together tight. Blake reached out and flicked back a strand of her vivid hair.

'Of course.'

Clare didn't like this new, reserved attitude.

'When did you get back?' she asked stiffly, like a stranger.

He rubbed a hand across his forehead.

'Late last night,' he replied, as she moved toward the kitchen.

'Coffee?'

When he shook his head, she hesitated.

'Everything work out in Darwin?'

'We did what we could.'

In his present state of exhaustion, Clare hesitated to ask anything of him.

'Feel like a short drive?' she asked.

'Sure.'

She tossed him a bunch of keys from her handbag.

'Back out my car while I get my coat. I have a surprise for you.'

When she was ready, Clare tossed her briefcase into the back seat of her car and slid into the passenger seat beside Blake.

'Into town.'

As they drove around the winding lake road, a latent tension brewed between them.

'How was your week?' he asked.

'I was so busy, time flew.'

Clare cringed as she lied.

'I'm much more comfortable with people in town now. There's Tracy at the general store, and Steve, the builder who carried out my office renovations. He invited me to dinner one night this week.'

Blake fell quiet for a moment, then said, 'Good.'

He swung the car into the main street and halfway along, Clare said, 'Here it is.'

Blake found a space, opened her door and retrieved her briefcase. As he handed it to her, their fingers touched and he pulled away as though stung. Clare stifled her disappointment at his transmitted message. He was being sensible and professional, easier for both of them. She unlocked the office and noticed that all the furniture had been delivered but not placed. She swept an arm about, proud of her new domain.

'Do you like it?'

The mushroom walls and burgundy carpet were a rich complement for her solid pieces of old timber furniture. It gave the office a comfortable, lived-in appeal.

'You've done well in a week.'

'It's going to need some re-arranging.'

Blake planted his hands on his hips, his dark eyes sparkling, his mouth edged with amusement.

'Need a strong pair of hands?'

He looked too tired to hold a cup of coffee let alone move furniture.

'Are you sure?'

'Think about it while I get lunch. I skipped breakfast. What would you like to eat?'

She shrugged then took the easy way out by saying, 'Anything hot.'

Clare changed her mind a dozen times about the office arrangement before Blake returned with food, a large container of fried rice and two paper cups of lemon tea. Her favourite!

She kicked off her shoes and sauntered as she forked into the rice.

'I'll have my desk over here, partly screened by a partition. It will give me privacy for my appointments but I can still see the general office. I'll need this space open,' she indicated the front of the shop, 'for client photographs and samples of their work, and the other partitions and desks I'd like along here.'

She indicated the far wall with her plastic fork. Blake's eyes didn't leave her as he sipped his tea. Aware of his gaze, Clare babbled on, nervous.

'I'll be interviewing staff this week so it will be great to have it all organised. I've been in touch with my Melbourne contacts to market local work. There's already a possibility of regular orders.'

It was working, being positive, ignoring Blake's sensual vibrations. Blake had only been away for days and already she felt vulnerable. Before long, he would be gone for good. She must learn to cope on her own and get used to life with him. A sharp ache knifed through her.

Blake gathered up the scraps of their lunch. Clare looked confident and decisive. She was one determined lady. An edge of tension lingered, understandable, getting a new business off the ground. Time for him to step aside and let her move on to the next phase of her life. Her success should have pleased him. Instead, he felt only an unusual heaviness in his heart.

'What are you thinking?' Clare asked.

'How proud of you I am.'

'Thank you.'

'I can leave soon,' he said gently.

Clare gripped the edge of the nearest desk and leaned against it. These were words she expected but didn't want to hear.

'When?'

'Next week.'

The bottom fell out of Clare's world.

'Fair enough. Do you have time for house hunting before you go?'

Responding to his raised eyebrows, she said, 'I'm buying my own place. I'd appreciate your help with the structural stuff.'

For a moment, Blake hesitated and she panicked that he might refuse.

'A home is a personal thing. Do you really need me?' he asked, blunt and unenthusiastic.

A loaded question, she thought but replied, 'Definitely.'

'All right, but it can't be today. I'm beat and I have paperwork.'

'Of course. Tomorrow?'

He nodded, and she pushed herself away from the desk.

'Let's go. You look terrible.'

'Thanks. I feel it,' he answered with a wry smile.

'You should forget your paperwork and go straight to bed.'

Clare was overcome with an image of Blake, ruffled and sleepy, beneath the covers. He eyed her strangely as he shrugged into his coat.

'You could be right. Anything else

you need to do here today?'

Clare shook her head.

'It can wait.'

They headed for her car. This time, Clare drove. They had barely left town when Blake's eyes drifted shut and she stole glances at him all the way home. At his cabin, she gently shook him awake. His sexy half-smile made her head spin and her heart tumble.

'Thanks. I owe you one,' he said as he opened the door and unwound his long legs from her car.

'OK if I call you after I've set something up with the real estate agent?'

He nodded and waved, already striding away toward his cabin.

Steve telephoned later to confirm his dinner invitation for Thursday night. Aware of the huge gap Blake would leave in her life after he left, Clare realised she needed to widen her circle of friends.

Watching the television news that evening, she ate a packaged Caesar

salad for dinner, disinterested in anything more substantial. She wondered if
Blake had eaten or was still sleeping.
He had only picked at lunch despite
claiming to be hungry. Tired and
apprehensive over the persistent nightly
noises, she double-checked all the
windows and doors, changed into her
pyjamas and went to bed. She would be
fine. Blake was back and only a
telephone call away. On that comforting
thought, she drifted off to sleep.

Unknown hours later, Clare shot up
in bed, woken by a noise that sounded
like shattering glass. Her heart
thumped. Above its pounding, she
heard movement and realised it was
inside the cabin! She froze, paralysed
with terror in her dark room. Had
Toley's men found her? Suddenly, the
past reared its ugly head and became an
unwelcome nightmare in the present.
She checked the red numbers on her
digital clock. Two-twelve. Her hand
searched blindly for the telephone on
her bedside table and Clare silently

groaned. She had forgotten to bring it in.

She stiffened and listened, afraid to breathe, feeling trapped and isolated. What if the person came into her room? Was it a stranger or someone she knew? Had they been watching her? Then something snapped inside her. Grit mingled with fear and burst into fury. She would not sit here and take this. How dare anyone violate her again? She had just started a whole new life and would not be intimidated. She gritted her teeth, determined to face whatever came.

Angry and shaking, Clare crawled quietly from bed. As she steadied herself on the bedside table, her hand felt a cold object. She explored it. Her heavy, silver-backed mirror, a treasure from her grandmother! Clare grasped it with a pang of regret. If it was ruined, it would be in a good cause! She crept from her room then edged from the bedroom and along the hall. Her sweaty hand helped feel the way along the wall while the other gripped the mirror handle.

At the living-room doorway, she paused, inched her head around the opening and gave her eyes time to adjust to the gloom. Faint moonlight helped. A shadowed figure moved furtively about, stripping shelves bare and opening drawers. Making so much noise, Clare suspected the person was an amateur. It couldn't be one of Toley's men. They would be professional, swift and silent.

Terrified of discovery or failure, Clare prayed and moved into the room, taking one soft step after another, ever closer. The burglar had his back to her. She hesitated behind him. Holding her breath, she raised the mirror above her head. The intruder must have sensed something. Suddenly, he turned, looming over her, his eyes wild. Startled, Clare screamed. Taking no chances, she closed her eyes and smashed the heavy weapon over the intruder's head. Glass fragments splintered over them.

The burglar let out a sharp cry. Holding his head, he staggered toward the kitchen and escaped through the back door. Stunned and shaking, Clare rejected pursuit. Injured, the burglar might not get far. Shaking, she fumbled for the lamp and clicked it on. The entire living area had been trashed. Numb with shock, she telephoned the police then Blake.

'I'll be there in five minutes,' he told her.

He made it in three.

6

Gasping, Blake burst through Clare's cabin door in a navy tracksuit and unlaced sneakers. Dropping his torch, he reached out for her.

'Are you all right?' he barked, grasping her by the shoulders.

Trembling, she nodded, secure in his presence.

'What on earth happened?'

Clare explained as he scanned the devastation. Police sirens sounded in the distance. He turned back to her and ran his hands over her face.

'Are you sure you're not hurt?'

'I'm fine.'

'Did you recognise him? His voice? Anything?'

'No. I didn't get a proper look in the dark but he didn't seem familiar.'

The sirens wailed louder.

'Let's wait for the police, see

what they find.'

Blake rubbed her arms to ease their shaking. When that didn't seem enough, he drew her against him and held her tight.

When the police arrived, Blake answered the door. Clare stepped over the mess on the floor and sank on to the couch. She retraced the night's events for the police as clearly as she remembered. Was Toley responsible for this or was it just a coincidence and totally unrelated?

Through everything, Clare was vaguely aware that Blake stoked up the lounge room fire, added more wood, made coffee all round and pressed a mug into her cold, trembling hands. He laid a blanket across her knees then sat beside her and wrapped a comforting arm about her shoulders.

'Anything stolen, Miss Rayne?' the officer asked.

Clare shook her head and drank more coffee, cupping her hands around the mug to warm and still them.

'I don't think so. The cabin is rented. The owners have an inventory.'

'And you say you've heard unfamiliar noises all week?'

Absently, Clare nodded, and Blake flashed her a formidable glare.

'You didn't say anything.'

'I was trying to be independent.'

'Probably casing the premises,' the officer said. 'There have been other break-ins in the area in recent weeks.'

Clare's spirits rose.

'We believe we know the burglar's identity.'

He rose and snapped his notebook shut.

'We'll catch him.'

Eventually, the last person left, and Blake closed the door.

'Sounds like it wasn't Guzzi after all,' he said and they exchanged a relieved glance. 'Why didn't you tell me about the noises?'

'You were at the other end of Australia,' she explained calmly.

'I should have been here for you.'

'No, you shouldn't,' she said, proud of her false detachment. 'And, anyway, how could you have helped from Darwin?'

'Come back, to be here.'

'Seriously?'

'Yes.'

'And done what?'

'Kept watch outside your cabin.'

'In the freezing cold, all night?' she chided.

'If necessary.'

Clare stilled, realising the extent to which Blake was prepared to protect her, a strange depth of commitment for someone who professed neutrality, and far beyond professional duty. Her senses dulled and she frowned, closing her eyes for a moment, feeling lethargic and warm.

'The coffee was laced, wasn't it?'

He nodded.

'Just a nip. You were in shock. I'm staying overnight.'

Too drowsy to protest, she sagged against his shoulder. Her head rested just beneath his chin. When she gazed up at him, bemused, she neither resisted the magnetism nor fought the urge to kiss. It was wrong but the most natural response in the world, and Clare didn't want the excitement and sensuality to end. But Blake moaned and pulled away.

'I shouldn't take advantage.'

'I know exactly what I'm doing,' she said softly.

'Right. So one of us has to be sensible.'

Clare pouted with amusement.

'Well, don't look at me, and anyway, why? Didn't you tell me once to grab every moment?'

'So I did.'

'Do you think I'll fall into a heap when you leave? I'm stronger and wiser now. I can handle anything, rejection, separation. You name it. I've become quite a master.'

Gently, Blake released her and rose from the couch, moving away from her to create distance and crossing to the picture window. Holding the curtains aside, he stared out into the inky darkness beyond.

'Clare, I'm a drifter. My work takes me all over the country, sometimes overseas. I go where I'm needed.'

He turned back to face her.

'You need stability now and I can't provide that.'

'Don't you care?' she whispered.

'Actually, I do.'

Clare's heart swelled with hope but just as swiftly sank with dejection.

'Then why can't you show it?'

'I just explained.'

Barely able to stand, she struggled to her feet.

'That's a cop-out. And you are so wrong about me, Blake Fielding.'

Her eyes glinted with anger as she staggered bleary-eyed into the hall and reappeared with an armful of sheets and blankets. She threw them at his feet and they landed in a crumpled mass on the floor.

'Sweet dreams, counsellor.'

'Clare!'

'Don't Clare me,' she hurled at him. 'You're no better than Toley.'

'I'd prefer to think I'm above his type.'

'Prove it!'

Blake shook his head.

'You're asking the impossible.'

Standing apart like enemies, Clare ached for him.

'Sometimes it's worth reaching for,' she said quietly.

She suspected it wasn't her emotions Blake was afraid of but his own. He had gained and earned her trust. Why couldn't he just let go and do the same for her? What held him back? Without another word, Clare whirled from the room, retreated down the hall and slammed her bedroom door. Miserable, she slid beneath the quilt. Sleep was impossible. Her mind spun with thoughts of the burglar's identity, the police questions, and Blake. Finally, the brandy took over and she fell asleep.

In the morning, Clare rose reluctantly from her warm bed and stretched. Still feeling lethargic and drained from the events of the previous night, she padded barefoot along the hall to the kitchen hoping Blake was still asleep. She didn't want to confront him before her first cup of coffee.

' 'Morning.'

Clare froze at the kitchen sink and turned to see Blake reclining against the door. In his rumpled track suit, bare feet and ruffled hair, with a shadow of stubble on his face, he looked adorable and irresistible. She wished he would take the few steps across the room to bridge the distance between them but remembered his denial and toughened her resolve.

'I hope you slept badly.'

'Like a lamb,' he drawled. 'You look cute first thing in the morning.'

'Fortunate you can control yourself so well, then, isn't it?'

She smiled sweetly.

'I've had breakfast. Feel free to make

your own. Coffee's hot,' she added and nodded toward the percolator. 'And you're welcome to whatever else you can find.'

'Are you always this grumpy in the morning?'

His amusement irritated her.

'Only around you. Seems I'm allergic.'

She stalked off.

After her shower, Clare tucked a dressy dark green T-shirt into fitted cream slacks and cinched them with a tan belt. She was fixing her hair and make-up when Blake tapped on the door.

'Yes?'

He entered, carrying a tray with an omelette, toast and fresh coffee. Her nostrils flared and her stomach yearned at the sight of steam rising from the plate and the aroma of tasty food. She turned away.

'I told you, I've had breakfast.'

'No, you haven't,' he disagreed. 'You were barely in the kitchen five minutes before me. You hardly had enough time to brew coffee let alone cook anything.'

He set the tray on her bedside table.

'Besides, there were no dirty dishes in the sink. Eat.'

The telephone rang and Blake raised his eyebrows.

'Be my guest.'

Clare shrugged and continued with her make-up as he disappeared to answer it. She heard his murmured tones from the living-room but not what was being said. In his absence, she stole a few mouthfuls of food as she slipped into her expensive tan brogues. With a slice of toast between her teeth, she had just shrugged into a tailored jacket when Blake returned.

He leaned against the door frame, arms crossed.

'It was the police. They caught the burglar.'

Clare finished her toast and breathed a sigh of relief.

'Great. Criminals should be punished.'

They both knew she referred to Toley.

'It was a teenager. Just boredom and petty crime.'

Clare drew a tissue from its box, wiped her mouth and prepared to leave.

'You haven't finished.'

'I've had sufficient. Thank you.'

She breezed past him and went out into the living-room. Blake carried the half-eaten food to the kitchen and reappeared to see Clare fussing with her briefcase. He moved closer and laid a gentle hand on her arm.

'Clare . . . '

She moved away and he sank his hands into his pockets.

'I'll clean up this mess for you.'

He cast a gaze over the chaos in the room still looking like a windstorm had blown through.

'No need. I'll do it later. You have your own life as you so clearly pointed out. I don't think you should spend too much time here, do you?'

'Clare, this is about you as a patient,

not a woman. When I come into contact with people professionally, they have usually just suffered a major change or breakdown in their life. You're no exception. Things happen. People change.'

She understood the direction of his explanation.

'I agree but my relationship with Toley ended because he was a criminal, not because I couldn't go the distance. I've grown since then, I've learned, thanks to you. But you still believe I'm not a stayer, that I'd leave at the first sign of trouble.'

'No.'

'Then what?'

She stared at him, feeling hopeless, knowing something deeper than physical chemistry lay between them waiting to be explored.

'We're not analysing me here.'

'Well, maybe we should,' she said quietly. 'Maybe it's time you took a good, long look at yourself and heeded some of that advice you're always giving to others. After everything I've revealed about myself, you know the real me. I'm standing before you. I faced Toley. I did not quit. I survived. Surely that must account for something.'

She snapped her briefcase shut and looked Blake directly in the eye.

'I'm no coward. I don't back off.'

'I know all that.'

'Exactly, but I know nothing about you,' she said in frustration.

Immediately, Blake's expression went blank.

'You need to get to work,' he said.

'Getting too close, am I?' she challenged softly.

'I'll drop by later.'

Blake Fielding was not a man who succumbed easily to his emotions. Maybe it came with his territory, moving on, travelling light. But maybe it was something more and, if so, did she really have any right to know? Maybe she was kidding herself and didn't mean as much to this man as she thought.

She cast a despairing glance around the messy room. She hated housework whereas Blake, for all his nomadic lifestyle and alleged independence, had neatly folded his sheets and blankets on the couch and spoiled her with a cooked breakfast. The man was an enigma and no mistake. With a sharp pang, she knew she would be desolate when he left.

Starting again in a new life had been a struggle. Starting again without Blake might prove impossible.

7

Clare's first stop in town was the police station. She completed the formalities and signed an official statement. Her second stop was Mr Palmer, the real estate agent.

'I'm afraid there are few homes on the market at the moment, Miss Rayne, being winter and all.'

'I understand,' Clare said. 'I'm prepared to look at anything you have. Nothing fancy, just somewhere I can call home.'

He spread out details and photographs of three properties he considered suitable. Clare studied them and agreed all deserved inspection.

'Could I see them tomorrow?'

They arranged a time and she left.

Staff interviews all afternoon made the remainder of Clare's day fly. It was dusk by the time she ushered her last potential employee from the office and locked the door. Within moments of her arrival back at the cabin, Clare's telephone rang. She dumped her briefcase and kicked off her shoes.

'Hi,' Blake said. 'How was your day?'

He must have noticed her cabin lights go on. Clare curled up on the sofa.

'No gremlins.'

She kept her tone casual.

'Good. How are the interviews going?' he asked stiffly.

Clare steeled herself against the pain and said, 'I've narrowed my choices but still have a few more applicants to consider in the morning.'

'Good. Actually, I rang to ask you a favour.'

'Oh?'

'I'm having to have my vehicle fixed before I leave next week. Since my car will be out of action until I get the part, would you mind picking it up in town for me in the morning?'

'Of course not.'

Clare jotted down details of the spare part.

'Try the auto shop at the local garage. He carries a good stock.'

'All right.' Clare paused. 'Are you still available for house hunting?'

He hesitated and, for a moment, Clare thought he might back out.

'Sure.'

'Tomorrow?'

Another pause. Enough to give the impression he was reluctant.

'I'll need about an hour to replace the part. After that, I'm all yours.'

She wished! Silence stretched across the line.

'Are you sure? After our conversation this morning . . . '

'Clare, nothing can change.'

Deeply disheartened by his words, she said, 'I know where I stand.'

'I can't give you what you need right now.'

'If you keep saying it, you might even convince yourself.'

'Clare, don't make this harder.'

She ignored the tension.

'Is one o'clock OK tomorrow?'

Another revealing pause.

'Sure.'

Clare hung up but kept her hand on the phone, thoughtful. Their time together would end soon. She didn't expect happily ever after, just a chance to share her happiness and love for him.

Next morning, armed with the note describing Blake's car part and having no idea what it looked like, Clare drove into town. She found the auto shop and pulled into the kerb. Inside, a salesman attended another customer at the counter so she waited.

Presently, another man entered the shop in overalls and a tattered jumper, sporting an unshaven, surly face. He stood beside her, his size intimidating. She didn't recognise him although she had come to know many of the locals in recent weeks. The knitted hat he wore was pulled well down over his head and ears. It could have been against the cold.

Clare grew uncomfortable. Inexplicably, his presence triggered an image, a memory. Her hands grew sweaty, her breath shallow and her head pounded. Somehow she got a grip on her paranoia. He wasn't stalking her. She was being foolish, her thoughts unreasonable. Stepping forward to be served, she stuttered out her request for Blake's car part to the salesman who eyed her behaviour strangely. Pushed by a sense of urgency, she paid for it and fled the shop.

Clare's hands shook as she unlocked her car, then sped from town. Breathing fast as she drove, she wondered how long these outbursts of suffocating panic would continue. She groaned impatiently, wanting to be free, now. She wanted it to be all over, now. She struggled to be rational but knew complete peace would only evolve with time.

She was barely calm when a red sports car appeared in her rear vision mirror and tail-gated her. Her hands tightened on the steering wheel. Toley had driven one exactly the same! Terrified, she cringed as it pulled out, overtook her and moved ahead. Anxious to reach the cabin, Clare accelerated, ignoring the speedometer when it passed the speed limit.

Nightmares came in threes, it seemed. As if the surly man in the auto shop and the red sports car were not enough, the next thing, a police car, lights flashing, siren wailing, drew alongside, the officer flagging her to stop. Shaken, Clare pulled over and wound down her window. As the young officer strode toward her, she wanted to crawl under the seat. It was the policeman from the burglary the other night.

'Miss Rayne!' he said in mutual recognition, clearly surprised.

She nodded, her tongue dry, her head pounding with anxiety.

'Everything OK?'

'Yes,' Clare forced out with a pleasant smile.

'Still a little upset from the break-in?'

'I guess.'

'Do you realise you were speeding?'

'Was I really?'

Clare pretended ignorance.

'Could I see your driver's licence, please?'

Again, Clare supplied proof of her new identity. The more often she did it, the easier it became, another hurdle overcome.

'I'm really sorry about this. I don't normally speed.'

'I'll make allowances this time, Miss Rayne, and just give you a warning.'

After a parting word of caution, the policeman left. Tears pricked Clare's eyes and she blinked them back. She didn't usually indulge in self-pity but today's events had caught up with her. She blew her nose and drove on to Blake's cabin to find him working underneath his four-wheel drive.

'Here's your universal what's-it-name,' she muttered.

At the sound of her voice, he slid out

from under the vehicle and smiled.

'Thanks. I appreciate your trouble.'

Noticing her distress, Blake stood up, wiped his greasy hands on a rag and gripped her by the shoulders.

'Hey, what's the matter?'

'Just my crazy imagination.'

She wanted to burst into tears again but stubbornly resisted.

'What happened?'

'There was this guy in the auto shop who looked suspicious. Of course, he wasn't, but I panicked and fled. Then this sports car tailed me, and then there was this policeman.'

She waved an arm in mid-air as though no explanation was adequate.

'I feel such a hysterical idiot.'

'Oh, Clare, honey.'

Blake scooped her into his arms.

'You're no such thing.'

She felt his warm breath against her hair as he spoke.

'Remember what I said?'

'I'll have lapses,' she mumbled, feeling a burden but soaking up the

132

attention anyway. 'Sounds like this was one of them.'

They drew apart and she blinked at him through wet lashes.

'I lost it.'

'You'll be ready for it next time. The attacks will happen less, then they won't happen at all. Are we still on for house hunting?'

He skilfully diverted the conversation.

'What am I going to do without you?' she whispered.

'Get on with your life,' he said.

Always practical. Didn't Blake Fielding, the man, ever let down his emotional guard? Clare knew she would encounter bad times and be ready for them. But would she ever be ready for life without Blake?

★   ★   ★

'Bit big, isn't it?' Blake declared.

'No,' Clare said. 'After living in a small terrace for years, I want space.'

They stood together on the pavement

inspecting the first property for sale while Mr Palmer unlocked the house.

'It's very . . . suburban, isn't it?' she noted, running a critical eye over the traditional brick home.

It was an unbelievably low price but then this was the country and cheaper living. The house was closer to town than the cabin, tucked comfortably among others of a similar style in a residential area, away from the lake, without her precious view. They went indoors but fifteen minutes later, Clare knew it wasn't right. It was too luxurious and too perfect. Sensing her disinterest, the agent whisked them away to the next property.

They pulled into the driveway of a cosy bungalow with French windows and a cottage garden. This house looked delightful but was it her?

'The furniture will be sold with the house,' Mr Palmer pointed out as they wandered the charming, small home. 'The elderly lady owner can't manage any more. She's moving into a retirement home.'

Clare trailed her fingers over the antique furniture.

'Seems ideal,' Blake said when he returned from an outdoors inspection.

Clare stared at him.

'Why?'

'It's established, not too big. You're a single, professional woman. You'll be busy.'

She shook her head.

'I'd prefer more room. Besides, this doesn't have the feel about it.'

'Feel?'

Blake frowned.

'That it could be my home,' she explained, 'like my terrace in North Melbourne. It was a dump when I bought it, but the moment I walked in, it had an ambience, a feel, a kind of potential of what it could become.'

As they departed for the final property, Clare glanced at Blake.

'Do you have a home?'

'No. I told you, I'm always on the move.'

'Live out of hotel rooms?'

'Mostly.'

Their conversation was interrupted as Mr Palmer pulled up before the last house, a stone and timber structure with an interesting shape, built amid bushland on a slight rise. A wide, timber deck stretched across the front and wrapped around the sides. The moment Clare laid eyes on it, something stirred inside her. She stifled her excitement as they alighted from the car and glanced over her shoulder through the gum trees. Because of its height, the house virtually had an uninterrupted dream view of the lake. Her anticipation soared.

Blake sauntered off outdoors as Clare and Mr Palmer went inside.

As they stood in the centre of a huge, open living area, he explained, 'The young couple who built it have separated and returned to the city. Houses this special don't often come on to the market. Of course, it is over your price range,' he mentioned discreetly.

Tactful as always, he left her to contemplate and browse. From where she stood, Clare's gaze tilted upward from the huge, stone fireplace to admire the exposed wooden beams that rose to form vaulted ceilings. Natural light streamed in through floor-to-ceiling windows that afforded magnificent views of the bushland and lake. Downstairs accommodated all the living and utility areas. Upstairs, were four large bedrooms, bathrooms and a delightful studio attic — perfect.

When Blake returned, he found her reflecting in the centre of the enormous lounge.

'It's wonderful,' Clare's voice echoed around the interior as she slowly circled the polished, timber floor. 'Such a restful place to live.'

'The kitchen looks like a chef's dream but you don't cook,' he teased.

Clare wrinkled her nose.

'Neither do you. I can learn.'

'The back yard extends into the bush,' Blake commented.

Clare thought of Dan's and Mary's three boys and Steve's children. Great for kids to play. She crossed her arms and contemplated a large wall that swept up to the cathedral ceiling.

'I could cover this entire area with paintings, traditional aboriginal art, bush landscapes, maybe some sailing ships,' she enthused.

'You're serious about this place?' Blake sounded surprised.

'I know it's expensive,' Clare said, 'but I can manage it.'

She crossed the room and pushed open the doors on to the deck.

'Doesn't this view blow your mind?'

She leaned over the rails, inhaling the crisp air as a breeze drifted up from the bushland below.

'I think I've found myself a home,' she beamed at Blake.

'You don't want to think it over?'

Clare shook her head.

'I know it's right.'

'I'd need time to make an important decision like this,' he admitted.

He forced himself not to show the enthusiasm for this house that had welled in his chest the moment he saw it. She was right. It did have a feel about it. You could raise a family here, not that he had ever given the idea much thought. He had been a drifter too long and doubted he could change. He edged away from her side to create a distance between them.

'Thanks for helping me today,' she said. 'I appreciate it.'

'You've come a long way, Clare Rayne. You should be proud.'

Dark eyes met hazel. Captivated, she closed the space that he had deliberately widened between them moments before. Because Clare was barely a heartbeat away and had become his irresistible weakness, Blake's control came unstuck and all of his ironclad good intentions vanished. She was an enticement and no mistake. Knowing he shouldn't, he leaned over and kissed her. It was bitter and sweet, pleasure and pain.

He kissed her again, deeper, slipping an arm around her trim waist, dragging her close. Then he stopped abruptly, forcing himself to shut down his passion. Clare gasped, stunned when he broke away.

'That proud of me, huh?'

'Sorry.'

'I shouldn't give you the wrong impression.'

She composed herself with a deep breath. She must learn to stifle her emotions so she didn't get hurt. Unfortunately, it was already too late.

'I'll go find Mr Palmer.'

Back in town, Clare signed the contract of sale in the estate agent's office and emerged thirty minutes later to find Blake lounging against her car. He raised the bottle of wine and two plastic glasses in his hand.

'I bought something to celebrate. What say we take it down to the lake?'

'Sounds like heaven.'

Greedily, she grasped every moment in his company. Because it was a mild evening, they sprawled out on a blanket on the foreshore. The lake was spread out like a vast sheet of glass, unmarred by a single ripple. Trees, sky and clouds all reflected in perfect mirror image in its dark waters. Blake poured the wine and raised his glass in a toast.

'Here's to your new home and your new life.'

Trying to be positive, she clinked his class.

'And success in business.'

They eyed each other in awkward silence. Clare was utterly bewildered that Blake could kiss her so passionately and then just walk away. He obviously had demons of his own to purge. Whatever they were, she wished he would deal with them and set himself free. She yearned to be nosy and pry but knew he would just clam up like a shell.

He was being so cool, she wanted to scream. Pretending interest in the lake view, she hugged her knees and drank more wine to numb her emotional ache. The sinking sun had grown large and red, spreading a broad golden pathway across the water.

'Thank heavens I won't lose this view when I move,' she breathed.

She took consolation that a small measure of peace existed somewhere in her life, if not in her heart.

'I leave Sunday,' Blake announced, not looking at her.

Clare's mind counted down the minutes, the hours in the few precious days until he was gone.

'How about a farewell dinner Thursday night?' he asked.

Clare realised she must refuse.

'I'd love to but Steve and his family have invited me over for dinner.'

'When are you free?'

There was an unusual curtness in his tone.

'Any other night.'

'Saturday?'

Clare nodded.

'That would be fine. Where are we going?'

'Dress up and leave your hair down,' he drawled. 'Let's make it a night to remember.'

Clare burned at his dare.

'All right,' she said nervously.

As twilight chilled the air, they finished the wine, folded up the rug and walked back to their cabins. Despite a thrill of expectation over their Saturday night dinner date, Clare also felt miserable because it would be the last time she would ever see Blake.

On Thursday night, Steve and Karen welcomed her when she arrived at their home. Married barely five years with two sons, a toddler and preschooler, theirs was a lively, young family.

They served themselves from huge bowls of food on the table, chicken casserole, rice and a dish of steamed vegetables. Baby Michael sat in a high-chair, swinging his short, chubby legs, cramming food into his mouth with his fingers. Jake joined Clare on her side of the table, asking a stream of non-stop questions.

With the five of them all seated around the table, Clare was reminded of Dan and Mary and their boys in Melbourne. Maybe she could brave it and visit them, and was surprised to discover the thought of returning to the city no longer caused her a single qualm. One by one, her past anxieties were being slowly dispelled, except for a nagging, deeper fear — losing Blake.

8

Clare knew she couldn't sit still for two days until her dinner date and last meeting with Blake on Saturday. Her new business was organised and staff chosen so, on an impulse on Friday morning, she made some telephone calls, packed a few essentials and jumped into her car.

She enjoyed the winding roads through beautiful countryside along the Princes Highway, the main artery to the city. After a few hours, Clare navigated Melbourne traffic to Dan's and Mary's home in the Dandenong Ranges on the city's eastern fringe. She had barely stopped in the driveway when Mary, with a beaming smile on her familiar, round face and brown hair cropped shorter since they had last met, appeared in the front doorway and flew from the house, four-year-old

Josh running to keep up with his mother.

'Clare,' she squealed, 'it's so good to see you. It's been months.'

She grabbed her estranged friend and crushed her in a hug.

When they broke apart, Clare said, 'At times I doubted I would ever see anyone I knew again.'

'Well, you're here and it's wonderful. You look fabulous.'

Clare blushed, suspecting her warm glow was for love of Blake.

'It's so peaceful in the country and I've organised a new business. Work has always agreed with me.'

Clare smiled down fondly at Dan's and Mary's youngest, his little nose wrinkled looking up at them, patiently waiting to be noticed.

'How you doin', Tiger? Remember me?'

Josh grinned up at her shyly.

'Hello, Auntie Clare.'

Flooded with a strange surge of maternal affection, Clare bent and lifted him into her arms.

'Are you going to come and visit me in my new home? It has a huge backyard right in the bush.'

Josh nodded eagerly. Is this what Blake meant by being a nester, Clare wondered. Her joy of children? Suddenly, a familiar cream and tan four-legged animal bounded into view. He gave an excited bark and wagged his tail. Clare gasped. After all this time, he remembered her! Setting Josh down, she bent to pat him.

'Sammy.'

She ruffled his silky coat and he nuzzled her affectionately in recognition. With misty eyes, Clare rose and looked up at Mary.

'You took him for me.'

Her friend nodded, grinning.

'You don't mind?'

'No. He's happy and loved. Thank you.'

'My dog,' Josh said, wrapping his short chubby arms with possessive affection around the dog's neck.

And so he was, now. Clare noted the attachment between them, making it clear this was now Sammy's home.

Mary linked arms and led her into the guest room.

'I was so excited when you phoned. Dan's on duty until late but he'll be home as soon as he can.'

Later, they sipped coffee in the conservatory that overlooked an extensive, paved terrace at the back of the spacious, rambling house. Josh had raced outside to ride his bike and Sammy loped excitedly around him.

'So, how's your counsellor?' Mary asked.

'Actually, I'm finished my sessions and he leaves in two days.'

She felt a twist of pain.

'But you don't want him to go,' Mary said gently and her steady gaze made Clare uncomfortable.

With shaky hands, Clare set down her coffee mug.

'His work is his life,' Clare said, trying to disguise her sorrow.

'Some life,' Mary said bluntly, honest as always.

'Each to his own. That's how the man chooses to earn a living. He's free to do as he pleases.'

Clare shrugged, puzzled why she defended a man who refused to admit his love. Mary leaned forward, concerned.

'You're not going to get hurt again?' she asked her friend.

'Absolutely not.'

Clare forced a light laugh.

'Heart of stone.'

At the moment, it felt like it.

'But you jumped right in anyway?'

'I didn't plan it, Mary. We can't always do that with our feelings.'

'Don't I know it,' her friend sympathised. 'Dan hit me like a brick. You couldn't have backed off?'

'Difficult. We saw each other every day and it just . . . happened.'

Mary meant well but Clare felt despondent. She had come here to escape this very subject.

'Mind if we skip this?' she said.

'Sorry. Didn't mean to pry.'

Mary sensed her mood.

'Just take care, OK?'

She patted Clare's hand and rose from the table.

'Dan and I worry about you. When Fielding leaves, promise you'll get on with your life?'

Clare nodded but it was a hollow promise. She knew she would feel empty and half alive without Blake. Even though their friendship hadn't worked out as she hoped, she would never have forsaken the joy of knowing him, not for a second. No-one could take away precious memories.

In the kitchen later, Mary retrieved a large dish of baked vegetable ravioli from the oven and set it to cool on the bench. She removed her oven mitts and began preparing a tossed salad. In amusement, Clare watched Josh riding the same route around the brick pathways, Sammy playfully nearby, until she realised she was the focus of

Mary's observation. She dragged her gaze away from the happy outdoor scene.

'What?'

'You've changed,' Mary answered.

'How?'

'You used to be such a live ball, never still. You're so much quieter.'

'Toley knocked out my stuffing,' Clare said wryly. 'I'm working on it.'

Forcing an enthusiasm she didn't feel, she explained all about her new business, the house and the townspeople she was beginning to know.

'I could never return to such a stressful lifestyle permanently so I expect you and Dan to bring the kids to visit.'

At that moment, the two older boys returned from school effectively ending their conversation. Clare caught up with all their news and, more importantly in a male household, their league football teams and how well they were performing this season, a hot topic with finals looming.

Soon after dark, and with impeccable timing, Dan arrived just as dinner was about to be served.

'How's my girl?'

The burly, six-foot policeman embraced Clare in a bear hug.

'She's in the kitchen getting dinner,' Clare laughed in reply, as they ambled down the long, wide hallway. 'And I'm fine.'

'You're looking great, kiddo.'

'I feel it.'

She hesitated.

'Thanks for sending Blake.'

Clare only wished she could mean it personally as well as professionally.

Dan grinned.

'Looks like it was worth it. You're glowing.'

Clare wondered how she managed to look externally alive when she felt so miserable inside. Self-conscious, she raised a hand to her face.

'Must be all that country air.'

A trio of sons stampeded down the hallway to claim their father and Clare was grateful for the interruption. She retreated into the kitchen and helped Mary serve dinner. It was a noisy meal, friendly and informal. Afterwards, Dan and Clare did the dishes while Mary bathed Josh, and Chris and Ben did homework. Later, the three adults settled in the lounge with coffee.

'How do you know Blake?'

Clare eventually gathered the nerve to ask Dan, curious.

'Through Dave MacKenzie. Dave was a police psychologist but resigned five years ago to go into private practice. Fielding's his partner.'

'Ah, so that's the connection. Mac being short for MacKenzie?'

Dan nodded.

'Do you know much about Blake?' Clare went on.

'Don't you?' Mary asked. 'You've had close contact with him for weeks.'

'He evaded any personal questions and made it quite clear that I was under the microscope, not him.'

'Mac mentioned that Fielding's the

strong, quiet type,' Dan said. 'Takes his work seriously. You'd be his first priority, no matter what he was feeling. Then again, maybe he's just plain stubborn.'

'You could be right.'

Dan reached over and squeezed her hand.

'Sorry if I got you into something, kiddo.'

'He is appealing,' she admitted wryly, 'but you helped me get on with my life through him and I could never resent you for that.'

A knowing twinkle entered his eyes as he sat forward eagerly.

'I have some information that will definitely brighten your day and probably your whole life.'

'I could handle some good news about now.'

Clare waited, intrigued.

'I've heard from reliable sources that a certain Anatole Guzzi is in big trouble and disgrace with his family back in Italy,' Dan revealed.

Clare harboured no sympathy for the man who had ruined her life.

'I'm not surprised. He robbed them of a fortune.'

'Which he'll be forced to repay.'

'How? He's bankrupt and in prison,' she said with a frown.

Dan smiled.

'Word's out that the minute he's released, the family wants him back in Europe to work off his debt. Years away, I know, but they'll wait.'

Clare understood the implication.

'That should keep him busy for the rest of his life.'

'Exactly,' Dan said and flashed her a satisfied grin.

'Out of Australia?' she asked hopefully.

'In all probability, he won't ever be allowed back into the country. You can safely regard Anatole Guzzi as history, Clare.'

In disbelief, Clare shook her head and pressed a hand over her mouth. She felt as if a ton weight had just been lifted from her shoulders.

'That's the best news I have ever heard in my entire life.'

She jumped from her seat and gave Dan a crushing hug.

'Oh, Dan, thank you. Now I can really get on with my life.'

'Thought you'd be pleased.'

'I'm so proud you were responsible for putting that bum in jail, Clare,' Mary said.

They all burst out laughing and proposed a toast, drinking it with the last of their coffee. Later, after the excitement and happiness had subsided, Clare headed for bed. Lying alone in the dark guest room, she contemplated Mary's and Dan's family. So much love and harmony filled their home but she despaired she would ever find it for herself. She rolled over and snuggled into the covers, looking forward to returning home next day. Before she fell asleep, the annoying thought crossed her mind that she had learned nothing more about Blake.

Saturday morning, Dan wasn't on duty so everyone slept in. They all dawdled over a late breakfast, eating toast and jam, and stacks of Mary's famous pancakes. Totally relaxed, Clare savoured every moment.

Late morning, Dan drove Chris and Ben to football and Mary disappeared to make beds and begin loads of washing. Josh brought an armful of clothes into the warm kitchen and Clare dressed him. With sunshine streaming in through the multi-paned French windows, he dragged out a book. They settled into the cosy, padded kitchen window-seat together, overlooking the back garden, and she read him a story. Tucked inside her arm, he turned the pages when she told him.

This, Clare knew, was what she was ready for in her life — a family, kids. But you needed a man to share it all with. She swallowed back hard against tears. Darn Blake Fielding. She wished she had never met him.

After lunch, Clare reluctantly said a quick goodbye, especially to Sammy, and was soon speeding back along the highway. The more she drove, the more it felt like coming home. It was early evening when she finally turned her car into the driveway alongside her cabin. Irresistibly, her thoughts drifted to Blake and she wondered how he had occupied these past two days. Had he tried to contact her, or missed her?

Clare bathed and dressed for their dinner date, leaving her hair down as instructed. The knitted black dress she chose flowed softly over her slender body to flattering effect. She did look rather svelte, she admitted, even to herself. Blake had hinted their evening would be special. A night to remember, he had said, but she had no idea where they were going.

She had decided to make the most of it and gather some memories. When Blake was gone, that was all she would have — and that was all he had promised.

9

Blake arrived, too soon, and yet not soon enough. Clare's heart turned over at the sight of him. In a dinner suit, he was breathtaking but looked uncomfortable as though he would rather be in jeans and sneakers than formal clothes. He cast her a ravishing gaze and whistled softly.

'Black dress, stunning hair. If you were up for sale, I'd buy you.'

She kept her gaze steady and her voice low.

'I don't believe you're prepared to pay my price.'

He knew what she meant and looked uneasy.

'I don't know how I'm going to climb into your four-wheel in this outfit.'

'Not a problem,' was all he said.

Blake seemed in no hurry to leave so Clare offered him a drink. Soon after, there was a knock at the door. She wasn't expecting anyone else and rarely had visitors. Blake answered it and greeted two impeccably-dressed men in black trousers, white shirts and red bow ties. Through the window, she noticed a van parked in the driveway. What on earth was going on?

'Good evening, Mr Fielding,' one of the men said.

Blake smiled and nodded.

'Right on time. We're ready for you.'

'Shall we unload?'

'Please.'

Clare sidled up behind him.

'You know these people?' she whispered.

He nodded.

She glanced over his shoulder and read the writing on the van — Country Catering. Blake had arranged dinner for them here in the cabin, alone, in private! The men carried loads from the van to the cabin and back again while Blake gave strict instructions. A stereo system was placed discreetly in one corner. A crisp white cloth snapped open and fluttered over a small round table. Cutlery and a branch of thick white candlesticks were set upon it and a bottle of white wine nestled among ice in a silver bucket. Domed silver food containers were whisked into the kitchen.

When all arrangements were complete, the last man pressed a button on the stereo and soft, background music filled the air, leaving Blake and Clare staring at each other. He switched off the lights, lit a match and touched its flame to the candles. Alight, they enhanced the intimate atmosphere. The perfume from an exquisite arrangement of opening scarlet rosebuds surrounded them.

'Hungry?' he asked once the men had departed.

'Starving,' she admitted in a husky voice, still adjusting to her surprise.

He pulled out her chair and she slid into her seat. Blake poured wine.

'To each of us.'

He meant separately, of course, so Clare determined to enjoy their precious last time together. When they were ready to eat, Blake disappeared into the kitchen, refusing her offer to help, and personally attended her, making her feel special. Realising what was on her plate, she finally understood. He served filet mignon smothered in a mushroom sauce with a bowl of side salad. This was her reward dinner, his parting gift.

'Thought I'd forgotten, didn't you?'

Blake grinned, dragging his chair cosily closer so that their elbows almost touched as they ate. She tried to settle but with the man of her dreams so near and unattainable, it wasn't easy.

Blake's dark eyes captured hers when the music became slow, and he rose, holding out his hands, guiding Clare into the centre of the living-room floor to dance. Ironically, when he took her in his arms, her defences crumbled but her senses sharpened. Clare closed her eyes and gave herself up to the night, openly revealing her love for him.

'Tired?' he murmured, his breath caressing her ear.

'No. Just enjoying the music.'

Firmly held, her forehead rested against his chin, her face brushed his neck. She had no idea what heaven was like but surely this was close.

Blake had held plenty of women in his arms during his lifetime but he had known from the first day they met that this one was special and threw him into turmoil. Holding her was restrained torment. Perhaps it was wrong to torture them both. He should have left sooner, but it was worth the agony just to hold her and be with her one last time.

He resented the music's end for he was obliged to release her. When he retreated to the kitchen, Clare used his absence to fan her hot face with a table napkin and breathed deeply to steady her racing heart. He returned with a generous slice of her favourite chocolate cake and one spoon.

'Aren't you having any?'

'I'll watch you.'

Sensually, he fed her each mouthful. Just when she had reined her feelings under control, Clare's temperature rose again. Aching with yearning, she wished he would kiss the cream from her lips and end this longing inside. But, of course, he didn't. His passion, too, was miraculously leashed.

Eventually, Clare shook her head and laughed.

'I couldn't possibly eat another bite.'

She held her breath as Blake brushed away a daub of cream clinging to her lips, exploding her fantasy into life.

'I do believe you're flirting, Mr Fielding.'

'Did I ever suggest I didn't find you attractive?'

'Not that I recall,' she admitted, 'but I thought I was off limits.'

'Not tonight.'

'Why not?'

'Because, technically, you're no longer my patient. We're a man and woman having dinner.'

'What if I want more?' she dared him, teasing.

'Then you'll have to learn not to be greedy. I warned you, remember?'

In one easy movement, he stood up, removed his jacket and tie, and slung them over the back of his chair.

'Let's work off some of those calories, shall we?'

Who was she to object or resist? As they danced, Clare knew a rush of sweet pleasure in his arms again. Their cheeks touched, their lips a whisper apart. When the agony could no longer be borne, instinct made Blake lower his head even as Clare tilted her face to meet him. As his lips swept hers, making her feel thoroughly possessed, she melted into him, all bounds released, the kiss dissolving all sane thought.

She wound her arms around his neck, absorbed in the feel and taste of him. She could never have enough of this man. Tonight was painfully sweet, sharpened by the knowledge of parting. As always, it was Blake who ended the kiss but when they broke apart, she caught the confusion in his gaze with only rueful satisfaction, knowing she felt the same.

'Take me with you,' she whispered.

Blake held her away from him.

'I'm never in the same place more than a few weeks.'

'I love to travel,' she pleaded, a hopeless ache curling through her.

'You'd want kids.'

'Then we'll settle.'

'What if I can't?'

Clare grew thoughtful, conscious of the concern behind his words.

'Is that your fear?'

She wanted to smooth the obvious distress causing his frown. Blake shook his head and became distant again.

'I shouldn't have kissed you,' he said, clearly annoyed with himself.

Suffering fresh confusion and disappointment, Clare backed away. It really was all about to end. For whatever reason, Blake was afraid to entrust his love to her. She rubbed her bare arms in despair. Why had she foolishly grasped at the slender hope that something, anything, would change?

'Can I contact you when I get back?' Blake asked.

Clare yearned to concede but felt resentful.

'You expect to breeze in and out of my life at will? That's unfair and I don't know how you can ask it of me. I don't see the point, do you?'

Obviously stunned by her refusal, he said curtly, 'It's up to you. You're calling the shots.'

'No, Blake, you are. Any time you want to change the rules and play fair, the decision is in your hands.'

The intense romantic mood between them was broken and their evening fell apart. Had it only been a fairy tale, Clare wondered, a few beautiful hours drawn from her imagination. She grew frustrated at Blake's stubbornness even as he shrugged back into his dinner jacket. Equally lost and desolate, they stared at each other across the room.

'Clare, please don't hate me.'

'Too late,' she muttered.

She couldn't survive on promises. She wanted the real thing, nothing less. If he would fly free of his inhibitions without the guarantee of a safety net, she would be there to catch and support him if he fell. That was what commitment to each other was all about but Clare sensed it would be useless to tell him.

Blake reached out to touch her but let his hand drop back by his side.

'I'm sorry I can't give you what you need, Clare.'

'Are you?' she said bleakly.

'We've grown close, Clare. I won't deny that and I have special feelings for you.'

Upset but stubbornly refusing to cry, Clare couldn't respond.

Sensitive to her anguish, Blake said softly, 'I have a present for you.'

He disappeared outside and returned

carrying a large, wicker basket.

'Open it.'

Intrigued, she lifted the lid. Inside snuggled a brown puppy with floppy ears and her heart melted instantly.

'I know he won't replace Sammy but I thought he would be company for you in that big house of yours.'

She picked up the wriggling bundle and cuddled it. How could Blake be so thoughtful and cruel at the same time?

'It's too small to be a guard dog. What is it?'

'A bitser,' and at Clare's questioning glance, he added, 'Bits of this and bits of that. I found him at the RSPCA.'

Clare laughed despite her damp eyes and shaky emotions.

'Then that's what I'll call him, Bitser.'

The pup struggled in her arms and licked her face.

Blake flicked a business card from his wallet.

'This number will get Charlie at the

office. She always knows where to reach me.'

Clare stared at the small piece of paper, her only future connection with him. For a second, she panicked. How was she supposed to forget this man, the love of her life to whom she had entrusted her heart?

Blake hesitated, reluctant to make the first move, then spun around and was gone. She heard his four-wheel drive roar into life and the sound of its engine disappear into the night. Saved from the need to be strong her composure crumbled and she dissolved into quiet weeping.

Within weeks, Clare and Bitser moved into their new home. When two agonising months passed without so much as a postcard, a letter or even a telephone call from Blake, Clare was finally confronted with the abysmal depth of her loss.

Then one morning at the office, she received a fax. Her heart leaped at the cryptic message.

Join me, it read.

Once Clare survived the shock of hearing from Blake, her excitement tempered. The terms of his offer were obscure so the potential gift of happiness was marred with uncertainty. What exactly did he mean? And how could she find out without frightening him off again?

10

Blake leaned over the balcony of the Gold Coast apartment in Queensland he had rented for the duration of his current assignment, and looked out across the expanse of the Coral Sea.

After leaving Clare two months ago, he had flown to Darwin with Mac for debriefing with previous clients, then on to Papua New Guinea to the site of a mining accident. Now, he was back and free in two days. For his entire absence, day and night, there wasn't a minute in any day since they parted that he hadn't thought about Clare.

Try as he might, he couldn't forget her. No other female had ever made him feel like sticking around. This woman did. Overwhelmed at the time, he fled! But within days, he had been wanting to see her, touch her, be with her. When his need had not dimmed,

Blake knew he was in trouble.

He looked down at the paper in his hand and read Clare's fax again.

Come and get me, he read, then went inside to reply.

Clare paced her office meanwhile. Waiting was unbearable. If Blake refused her challenge, she might as well hibernate to the Antarctic. The thought of finding someone else was absurd. He had ruined her for any other man. Suddenly, the fax machine whirred into life and she pounced on it. Blake's answer read, **What's the deal?**

Yes! Clare wanted to scream with delight. With shaking hands, she wrote, **House, kids and the dog.**

She hesitated to send it. Her entire future hinged on his reply but she wouldn't be anything less than honest. She crossed her fingers as the paper slid into the machine.

Blake made her wait overnight. The man obviously needed time. All the same, she grew impatient. He'd already had two months. How much longer did he need?

First thing next morning, he sent, **I'm not house trained.**

If there was a moon, she would have jumped over it. She had him thinking. At least it was a definite maybe!

I trained Bitser, I'll train you, she replied.

He immediately faxed back, **I love a strong woman.**

Tears filled Clare's eyes. He had never mentioned that word before.

But do you love me?

Clare's fax machine remained terrifyingly silent for the rest of the day.

That evening, she heard a vehicle pull up outside and heavy footsteps clump on the entry porch. Clare looked up as Bitser gave an excited yap and her front door was flung wide. One look at Blake there and Clare knew he was her destiny. She also saw the doubt on his face and wished she could make it easier for him, but this was a decision he must make alone.

'We need to talk,' he said softly.

'I'll give you coffee and thirty minutes' conversation,' she said teasingly.

Blake's smile knocked the air from her lungs.

'I'll need something stronger than that.'

With trembling hands, she poured him a brandy. He accepted it and swallowed the lot in one gulp, then prowled back and forth.

'I've been on the move for fifteen years,' he said, almost to himself. 'I don't want to let you down. I can't promise I can settle.'

Time to confirm it was all or nothing.

'This would be a home not a motel, and certainly no prison,' she responded carefully.

'I'd like to try,' he said and stopped his pacing.

'That's all I ask,' she assured him softly.

He shook his head, standing astride, hands on hips.

'House, kids and a dog. It terrifies me.'

Clare shrugged.

'I'm available for counselling on that, day and night,' she added in a husky voice.

'Don't look at me like that,' he muttered, 'or we'll both be in big trouble.'

Then he closed the distance between them in two giant strides and the adoration and love in his eyes froze her where she stood.

'Clare, honey, I don't ever want to hurt you.'

'I'll take my chances,' she whispered.

'You've been through so much, you're everything to me. I want to share with you what my grandparents had.'

Clare frowned and he explained, his expression intense.

'They were soul mates. What they had was for ever. I'm not sure I can give you that.'

Her heart swelled at the depth of his hopes for them, undoubtedly the reason for his hesitation to commit. What woman could ask for more?

'I'm sure your grandparents' marriage didn't just happen. I'll bet they worked at it. Nothing worthwhile is easily achieved.'

Clare reached up and smoothed her hand over his wrinkled forehead.

'Remember, you won't be alone. We would be in it together.'

Blake caught her hand and turned it over, pressing a kiss into the palm. He crushed them together and pleasure skimmed through her.

'I love you, Clare Rayne, with all my heart.'

She gave a long sigh of relief and sheer happiness.

'Oh, Blake, I love you, too, so much.'

'Marry me,' he said in a voice that was strong and sure.

'Yes. Oh, yes, please,' and suddenly inspired, she added, 'How about that little church across the lake?'

'Perfect. And after that?'

'I already have a house and a dog.

But I'll need your help with the kids.'

'Then we'd better make it official, real quick,' he muttered, dragging her closer against him again until she thought she would no longer be able to breathe, his embrace as tight and secure as she knew their future would be.

★　★　★

Despite the distraction of the large picture window in the little church overlooking the lake, Clare had no problem with concentration on her wedding day six weeks later, as they held hands and pledged their love.

Later, the reception at the house was shared with family and close friends. Blake's parents had driven down from Sydney and, with incredible organisation and determination, he contacted and assembled all six of his brothers and sisters and their families from across Australia.

Clare's sister, Susan, flew in from Hawaii, and her parents and brother,

David, drove from Adelaide. Dan and Mary and the boys stayed in the cabin. Mac and Charlie were there, too, and Clare's new office staff. She had felt ecstatic relief that, albeit with some caution, she could contact her family again and they could all be together.

Long after midnight, most wedding guests still lingered, thoroughly enjoying themselves, reluctant to leave. Blake dragged Clare into a corner.

'Let's get out of here,' he whispered.

'We can't leave our guests,' she protested.

'Want to bet?'

He swept her up in his arms and carried his bride off into the night.

★　★　★

One balmy, spring evening four years later, Mrs Blake Fielding stepped over the toys on the living-room floor of her house in the bush land overlooking the lake. Her husband gently nudged aside the drooling animal at his feet.

'Down, Bitser. You spoil him,' he teased his wife as he put his hands on her slim waist and drew her down beside him on the deck swing.

'Wasn't that your intention when you gave him to me? The girls adore him.'

'Alison settled?' he asked and she nodded.

Their oldest daughter had been given her mother's real name, connecting Clare's original past life to the present.

'Baby Hannah, too?'

She nodded and sighed, basking in the soft warm night, the love of her life beside her and a spread of stars overhead.

'This view never pales, does it?'

'Don't imagine it ever will,' he murmured.

After a while, Clare said, 'I know you dote on our daughters but wouldn't you like a son?'

He gave her a loving, if a trifle suspicious, glance.

'That a proposition?'

She flashed him a radiant smile.

'I've an early fourth anniversary surprise for you. We're having another baby.'

Blake wrapped both arms around his wife in a crushing squeeze.

'I said you were a nester,' he teased, his voice full of the special tenderness he saved for her alone.

'You don't mind another child?'

Blake shook his head.

'Absolutely not. This is a big house. We still have plenty of empty rooms.'

'Not feeling restless?'

He laughed softly.

'With all the activity around here and three women to keep me busy? No way?'

Clare rested a hand gently on her flat stomach.

'I just know it's going to be a boy,' she said with rising excitement, positive that starting again had been absolutely the best part of her life.

We do hope that you have enjoyed reading this large print book.

Did you know that all of our titles are available for purchase?

We publish a wide range of high quality large print books including:
Romances, Mysteries, Classics
General Fiction
Non Fiction and Westerns

Special interest titles available in large print are:
The Little Oxford Dictionary
Music Book, Song Book
Hymn Book, Service Book

Also available from us courtesy of Oxford University Press:
Young Readers' Dictionary
(large print edition)
Young Readers' Thesaurus
(large print edition)

For further information or a free brochure, please contact us at:
Ulverscroft Large Print Books Ltd.,
The Green, Bradgate Road, Anstey,
Leicester, LE7 7FU, England.
Tel: (00 44) **0116 236 4325**
Fax: (00 44) **0116 234 0205**

Other titles in the
Linford Romance Library:

THREE TALL TAMARISKS

Christine Briscomb

Joanna Baxter flies from Sydney to run her parents' small farm in the Adelaide Hills while they recover from a road accident. But after crossing swords with Riley Kemp, life is anything but uneventful. Gradually she discovers that Riley's passionate nature and quirky sense of humour are capturing her emotions, but a magical day spent with him on the coast comes to an abrupt end when the elegant Greta intervenes. Did Riley love Greta after all?

SUMMER IN HANOVER SQUARE

Charlotte Grey

The impoverished Margaret Lambart is suddenly flung into all the glitter of the Season in Regency London. Suspected by her godmother's nephew, the influential Marquis St. George, of being merely a common adventuress, she has, nevertheless, a brilliant success, and attracts the attentions of the young Duke of Oxford. However, when the Marquis discovers that Margaret is far from wanting a husband he finds he has to revise his estimate of her true worth.

CONFLICT OF HEARTS

Gillian Kaye

Somerset, at the end of World War I: Daniel Holley, unhappily married to an ailing wife and father of four grown-up children, is attracted to beautiful schoolteacher Harriet Bray, but he knows his love is hopeless. Daniel's only daughter, Amy, who dreams of becoming a milliner and is caught up in her love for young bank clerk John Tottle, looks on as the drama of Daniel and Harriet's fate and happiness gradually unfolds.

THE SOLDIER'S WOMAN

Freda M. Long

When Lieutenant Alain d'Albert was deserted by his girlfriend, a replacement was at hand in the shape of Christina Calvi, whose yearning for respectability through marriage did not quite coincide with her profession as a soldier's woman. Christina's obsessive love for Alain was not returned. The handsome hussar married an heiress and banished the soldier's woman from his life. But Christina was unswerving in the pursuit of her dream and Alain found his resistance weakening . . .